Working Bride

Patricia Pike

Other Books by Patricia Pike

The Bell Tolls Series
The Final Waltz

Air Whisperers of Nkandla

Non-Fiction
From Hallowed Land to Halloween

Children's Books
Rock Brothers
The Bat and the Glow Worm

Adult Colouring-in Books
Underground Rock Stars
Muddled Memories

Chapter One

Abigael Rabinowitz stared at her reflection in the mirror with dismay. Named for one of King David's wives in the scriptures, she always wondered why the family named her for a father's joy? Was she her father's joy? She wasn't pretty. In fact, no one ever said she even looked nice and at almost thirty years of age, she knew those compliments were never to be hers. The advert from the engineering magazine in her hand, she read it through once more to see if it really said what she thought it did.

"Wanted, girl with engineering or skills relevant to repair machinery to live and work in Africa. Client is looking for a woman to be his wife working alongside him in his endeavors to help with infrastructure to assist local people. Send application to…"

"Well, what the heck. Is this the chance of a lifetime to escape being at the beck and call of my parents and Joe." Abigael shuddered at the thought. Joseph was the very spoilt only son in a family of girls and in Spring, was due to step into the role of CEO of the ancestral business writing technical journals and instruction manuals.

No matter how many hours Abigael worked, and how many degrees she amassed, Joe was the golden boy in her father's eyes.

Her three sisters married and moved on with their lives. Only Abigael was left at home to care for her aged grandmother and demanding mother, as well as working a full day at the office. She loved those moments when a client phoned and requested her attendance at their factory to help with a new manual.

Sara and Rachel, her older sisters, were in marketing and the new digital divisions of the business and it was Abigael who was sent to appease difficult clients. Only the oldest sister strayed from the family firm and started her own business in fashion. Zlota fashion house and make-over business for the smart businesswoman. Zlota was a stylist for movie stars and celebrities and a household name. But Abigael doubted whether she could find a position working with her sister. Not even the amazing skills Zlota employed could change her from an ugly duckling into a swan.

She sent off her application to the address in the advert and waited. When the reply came two weeks later and an interview date and place, her heart jumped at thought. They would pay for her flight to Florida from New York, and she was booked into a hotel along with the other applicants. If Grandpa were still alive, she might have confided in him, but since his death a year ago, she knew her family would make fun of her.

And she told the family it was a friend's wedding in Florida she was attending instead of the truth.

Her mother fussed around making sure she was well dressed and insisted she have her hair styled for the journey. Abigael was used to these ministering efforts and allowed herself to be pushed and prodded into silly frilly dresses and crimped and cut into a style far removed from her usual.

"Maybe you'll meet a nice young man at the wedding, Abigael? A doctor or lawyer. We need a lawyer in the family." Her mother flicked her fingers through Abigael's hair, "A man who already has children and then you can be useful."

Abigael ground her teeth as she bit back any remarks.

Zlota visited with advice and when their mother insisted on the frills, she threw her hands up. "Enough, Muter. Abigael doesn't suit frills. Let me do my job."

But it was useless trying to change their mother's mind when she decided on what was best.

Zlota grunted in disgust and mumbled under her breath as she winked at Abigael. One thing she was grateful for was her three sisters being her best friends. Without them, life would be unbearable.

Grandma scowled at her. "Don't trust people, Abi. Remember what happened to me and your grandfather. It was a miracle we survived the death camp and escaped to America. A miracle.

And I think the day of miracles has passed for our family. Stay away from non-Jews. They don't understand our history."

Abigael nodded at this oft repeated admonishment. Grandpa would wink at her behind his wife's back and shake his head at his wife's negativity. He whispered quietly after each outburst.

"Life is a gift. Go out and live it to the full. We owe it to those of our family who never got the chance."

But Grandpa was no longer around, and it was with a heavy heart she packed her suitcase.

"I'm living my life, Grandpa. It's a gift and I don't want to waste it fighting with my brother and living a nightmare of regret. Grandpa, please give me your blessing and stay with me through this journey." She begged.

Arriving in Florida, she was surprised to see she was part of a cohort of twenty young women. There were those who were confident and others who were beautiful, but amongst them were the poor of heart. And it was to these women Abigael was drawn to.

Rosita from New Mexico was desperate to support her family of seven siblings and a single mother. Stephanie, from a small town in Ohio and was totally over-awed at the sights and sounds of a big city. She cowered in the corner until Abigael smiled and invited her to join the table with her and Rosita.

Then there was Peggy, the farm girl from Canada. And Margaret from Detroit, whose father worked on the car assembly line many years ago and taught her all he knew about engines. The beautiful girls gathered together as if attracted by magnets and a common heritage. But one of them looked over at Abigael and left her group to come and sit with them.

"Hi, I am Candice." She told them she once was a model and a small-time movie actress for a while. "But I met one too many men who thought they could control me, and I decided it was time to look for greener pastures. Not sure an arranged marriage is right for me, but I know how to change the oil in my engine, and I am a mean organiser."

She looked over at the group and asked each one who they were and where they were from.

The six women chatted away like old friends and when it came to dinnertime, it seemed natural to all gravitate to the same restaurant in the hotel. Jessica, one of the beautiful women, approached.

"Who is everyone bunking with? I have Rosita and would love to swap her out with Cherry. Do any of you have Cherry?"

She negotiated to have her roommate swapped from Rosita to one of her new friends.

"Let's all go and see a live show, ladies. My grandpa told me to enjoy life and today I'll take his advice." Candice said.

Abigael suggested "How about a show where the singer and backing singers dressed in nothing more than feathers and glue."

"Aww Abi, do they get paid to parade around in them feathers? Surely not." Stephanie frowned.

"Yes, Stephanie, they get paid lots of money to dance and if they have to wear feathers to do it, well, they don't seem to mind." She squeezed Stephanie's hand. "Now don't you worry about those ladies. Admire their gymnastic skills and forget about all the flesh on show."

Stephanie got over her shock and their lovely evening together, singing along to the popular songs and later sitting over cups of coffee and talking about the coming interviews eased her concerns.

"What do you think this man is looking for? I sure as heck don't want to be some old man's sexual plaything." Margaret commented and they all agreed.

"It is strange we haven't been given much information on our future prospective husband. What if he is smelly and ugly? Or mean and vindictive? I have met enough of those types of men and there is no amount of money to compensate for a nasty character." Jessica commented.

"Let's focus on the things we can control. We are all handy with a spanner and a screwdriver and let tomorrow take care of itself." Abigael warned.

None of the girls slept well. They sat bleary-eyed at breakfast the next morning.

A tall, blond man arrived with a clipboard in his hands. "Hi, I am Carl Young and I'm here to take you for a practical test. When you are ready, there is a bus waiting outside? And no, I'm not your prospective husband, ladies. I'm strictly non-marrying material."

He turned on his heel and ticked their names off the list on his clipboard as they climbed on the bus.

"It is not far, ladies. We've hired a workshop on the other side of town, and you will each be given an engine to repair. Overalls and tools are supplied, so you do not need to concern yourselves." The bus started up and pulled out.

Abigael glanced around the bus to see what everyone wore. She herself opted for a pair of denim jeans and a basketball shirt with Mickey mouse on the front from her last visit to Disneyland.

Her mother would be horrified she wasn't wearing something frilly. But there were plenty of the women who decided on revealing outfits of various styles.

Cherry wore a tiny pair of shorts and even Candice chose a frilly off the shoulder blouse to attend this first test. Abigael looked down at her kicks and smiled. At least the shoes were new and quite pretty. Zlota gave them to her for Hanukkah the year before. They were by far the best present she'd ever received. Bright blue toe caps and red heels with a daisy clasp to keep the laces from getting loose.

At the workshop, they were shown the changing area and could choose their own overalls. Jessica and her mates complained loudly about not looking their best in these simple outfits and checked their lipstick as Abigael and her group put their hair up in ties and removed earrings to prepare for the work ahead.

Benches with hydraulic pumps were laid out along with tools of all sorts. Abigael breathed a sigh of relief; she knew these pumps like the back of her hand. In fact, she wrote the manual for some of them and could recite their parts backwards and forwards.

There was the bright yellow pump she herself took to pieces often and a blue equivalent not much different. The rotary vanes and pump cartridges laid out alongside the main casing.

She walked up to a bench and touched the spare parts as if greeting old friends. Flex side plates and a rotor were in a bin along with cloths to clean them off. She noted there was no elliptical cam ring and frowned at this omission.

"Right ladies, as you can see, we've benches for you to work at. There are clamps and tools and a variety of spare parts. A large part of this job interview is geared towards you being a hands-on helper in this project. It's not for socialites or people who love the city life. If this doesn't appeal to you, you are welcome to leave. Your hotel will be paid for until Sunday night and we will hold no grudges if you depart at any stage. Right. You may start." Carl moved towards a staircase at the back of the work area. "I'm going to observe you from the office. Call if you need clarification on anything. But on the whole, we expect you to be a self-starter."

Abigael removed the bolts from the inlet cover after placing marks on the casing to ensure she re-assembled it correctly. There was nothing worse than doing everything right and then putting the wrong bit together. Next was the O-ring and so it continued until Abigael was confident all was working perfectly. It only took her a few minutes to complete the task. And then she looked around. Peggy and Margaret were happily re-assembling their units, but Rosita stood there with tears streaming down her face.

"Ah Rosita, it's not so bad. I can help you," Abigael promised.

Carl said nothing about helping each other and Abi was concerned to see her new friend so upset. "Look, it's easy. Take a photo of each stage with your camera and then you'll know exactly how to put it all back. One step at a time and you will be finished in no time at all."

"Abi, this doesn't look anything like what I've worked on before. Where do I start?" Rosita gasped.

Abigael smiled. "Use the clamps to make it easier to work on. Now take the bolts out."

As Rosita worked, she seemed to gain confidence and Abigael left her to her task.

Candice bit her thumbnail as she peered at the assembled mess on her bench in terror. Abi moved on and helped in the same way she with Rosita. Jessica wiped beads of sweat off her brow and again Abigael helped where she could.

"Why are you helping me, Abigael? You could be disqualified. And I'm not one of your mates, either. In fact, we haven't said two words to each other at all," Jessica said.

"Well Jessica, if I'm disqualified, then who cares? I don't think I stand a chance against you pretty ladies when it comes to this man choosing a wife. So, today I've decided I'll forget about the job and enjoy life to the fullest by helping others in need."

She laughed at the thought of how happy her grandfather would be with her attitude. When she smiled, the light in her eyes illuminated her face and changed her plain looks into something beyond beautiful. She looked the epitome of joy as she happily instructed and laughed along with the others.

In the observation office, Carl turned to his companion. "What do you want me to do? Should we disqualify her?"

Bryan Bond shook his head. "No, she's an interesting woman. She has no clue how special she is and seriously, did you see how fast she fixed the pump? I'm impressed."

"Ah yes, really speedy. But does it work? We will see. Do you want to come down and inspect the pumps with me?"

"Oh, heck no, Carl. I prefer to watch you work your charm on these unsuspecting females. If they respond to you by flirting, then I might have to disqualify them. I can't have my future wife in love with my business partner, now, can I?"

Bryan laughed at his friend as he placed his hands behind his head and watched the women below him working at the benches. They were almost finished with their tasks and Bryan shook his head in wonder. He hadn't expected to get so many women to reply to his rather cheeky advert.

It was the only way to ensure he married in the near future. All the girls he previously dated took one look at his primitive work area in the African bush and left in a hurry, never to return. How he came to decide on making it a business venture, started as a thought and then developed into an idea and seemed more interesting as the months went by.

He was lonely in the bush. There were the tourist volunteers to talk to, but it was not good business practice to sleep with random women and it was not his goal to put notches on his bedpost. He wanted someone he could share his life with. Someone to talk to about the things he found fascinating. Someone to share his passion for helping where he could for very little financial remuneration.

He started a Volunteer Working Holiday company focused on building infrastructure in areas where it benefited the locals meaningfully. Every few months, new tourists arrived with romantic visions of life in Africa. They thought lions roaming the countryside were amazing. Until they faced one of these predators threatening them. Some came with ideas of being the saviours to the wild savages and they were informed this was not the case.

The Chieftain they were presently working for was an Oxford graduate and not in any need of saving. She sourced financial help and funds from various charitable organisations and countries interested in a foothold in the area. She balanced out the needs and wants of her tribe with the hidden agendas of her benefactors. And there was no one as smart as Thandi Gumede. The tourists came to admire this amazing woman and her clear vision of what she wanted for her people.

Thandi was very supportive of Bryan and his quest for a wife and life companion. She even helped with the advert and suggestions on where to place them. Leaning forward now, he peered down at Carl as he wandered around the workshop asking questions. There were many beautiful women who seemed competent, but his eyes kept returning to Abigael. There was something drawing him to her. She stood next to an especially gorgeous woman, chatting and laughing with her in companionship. And yet the beauty of the other woman paled in insignificance as Abigael's eyes lit up.

"I wonder if Thandi will like you?" Bryan thought.

Carl returned and they went over the list of women as the ladies changed back into street clothes. When they were gathered once more, Carl announced who made the short list. He called out the five names they selected and apologised to the ladies who were not chosen.

"Not this time, ladies. Perhaps we could offer you other positions in the corporation if you would like to apply for the following jobs?" He laid out a sheet of job opportunities on the table and Rosita was quick to grab one.

Peggy and Margaret both made the short list, along with two other women they did not know. Jessica and Candice did not make the cut and they shrugged in resignation as they made their way to the bus. "After lunch, we will interview the ladies on the short list in a suite at the hotel. We will see you at about one o'clock."

He made his way back to Bryan, watching from a shaded part of the workshop. "Who do you think would be a good fit, Carl? I know who I like, but she will work with you too, so I would appreciate your input."

"Agh, now you are putting me in a difficult position, Bryan. It's you who has to sleep with this woman and seriously, none of them would make my short list. I like them leggy and dumb. The dumber the better."

Carl laughed. "I do like Peggy; she seems like she could live in the wilds of Africa. She grew up on a farm and I don't think she is shocked by much? Margaret is pretty, but she is more focused on car engines. Not much work for a mechanic where we are going. And sorry, but Abigael grew up in New York city. What the heck were you thinking of choosing her? She would freak out at what we put up with during our day-to-day lives. Living in a tent? And showering under the trees? Do you really think she would adjust?"

Carl shook his head and smiled at his friend. "Nah, she is a disaster waiting to happen."

"Maybe you're right Carl, but let us interview them all after lunch and see what comes afterwards?" They made their way to the hotel in their own vehicle.

Chapter Two

Some women left straight away for their hometowns and only a few of them stayed for a holiday at the company's expense. Rosita stayed and hung around Abigael as the lunch was served.

"Can you help me decide what jobs to apply for, Abi?"

"Sure Rosita. What skills do you have?" Over their plates of food, they went over the young woman's options.

"This job looks great for you. They are looking for a cook and a general dogs' body. It's in Namibia for six months, working at a wildlife foundation saving animals from poachers. You could do this. It will be a really fun thing to do. In fact, I might join you. I don't think I'll be chosen, and this looks perfect. Just imagine if we both got a position in the same place. I'd be happy to have a friendly face at work every day. I must get away from my brother, Joe, or else I'll go crazy." Abigael laughed. "Monkeys and meerkats are much better company than he is."

"Abigael, we can stay there for a year. Six months in Namibia and then maybe we could try our hand at something else? Let's see what else is available?" Rosita was so excited; it took a few moments before they noticed Carl hovering at their table.

"Abigael, we are ready for you. Let me take you up to the suite."

"Thanks Carl, we were making alternative plans if I don't qualify for this position." Abigael smiled as they made their way to the elevators.

"This is the weirdest job interview I've ever heard of. I can't say I've been to many interviews myself. I have worked all my life with my dad in Queens. But my brother is due to step into the business, and I can't imagine working alongside him. Agh, my worst nightmare. I would much rather shave a lion's mane than endure him being boss of me."

She looked up at Carl's surprised face. "Oh no, I don't expect in Africa you shave lion's mane. My grandfather used to explain his aversion to a task by comparing it to shaving a lion."

The door opened onto a suite of rooms. The lounge area beautifully furnished and, sitting on a long couch, was a tall man with wide shoulders and a serious look on his face. For a moment, Abigael stared at him, and then walked forward and introduced herself.

"Hi, I'm Abigael," she announced as she shook his hand and then took a seat opposite him. His eyes crinkled and her heart did a flip in her chest. Taking a deep breath to calm herself, she leaned forward slightly. Someone once told her she should mimic the stance of the person she wanted to impress. And she wanted to impress this man with the slight five-o'clock shadow and gentle smile. Her mouth quirked into a smile she couldn't suppress.

He cleared his throat. "I'm Bryan Bond and I'm the prospective husband and boss." He looked straight at her and she noted his slight grin in response to hers.

"Ah, so Carl here was a decoy? Okay, what do you want to ask me? I'm almost thirty years old and live at home with my parents and grandmother. I've worked in the technical manual fields all my adult life. I have a degree in journalism and another in mechanical engineering. Oh, and I'm a Jew, if you hadn't already figured out my ethnicity from my name?" Abigael knew she was rambling, but couldn't seem to stop.

She crossed her legs and leaned back in the chair, waiting for some response. Smiling at the look of surprise flashing across Bryan's face as he smiled back at her. His smile did something to her insides, a warm feeling in her stomach and she blushed at her wayward thoughts.

"First, why did you apply for this job? It is not your usual work situation. Surely you do not need employment with an impressive resume like yours?" Bryan queried.

"No, I'm not desperate for work. But I wanted something different from being the gofer to my brother and Father for the rest of my life." Abigael admitted.

"As to the marriage side of things? Well, I am a pragmatist and I know sometimes an arranged marriage is the only option. My Mum and grandmother hired a matchmaker at one time, but I was not what the usual Jewish man was looking for in a wife. And there was no way I was prepared to be a bargaining chip between families to secure alliances."

Bryan did not say a word except for the initial introduction, and it worried her she did not know who or what he was. This was the man who expected her to become his wife in all physical and emotional ways and so far, he needed to put his cards on the table for her to be comfortable.

"Can I ask a few questions?" She asked and Bryan nodded.

"Why do you need to employ a wife? Is there something I need to know about you. Is there something which might change my mind about undertaking this marriage?" Abigael blurted out.

Now it was Bryan's turn to laugh, and Abigael was pleased to hear it was not a snort or a guffaw. Rather, it was a pleasant sound, smiling at her reaction, her heart skipped another rapid little beat.

"I live and work in the African bush. There are few women who would find it ideal. I am looking for someone to share my life and passion with. I want someone I can talk to, who is intelligent and interesting. I have dated the pretty girls and the air heads and admit at the time it was fun, but I need more. I don't want to be a fifty-year-old man living all alone in a tent. If possible, I would like children and to achieve a family, I need a woman in my bed and my life. Hence the advert."

After a few more questions from both sides, Carl got up. "Thank you, Abigael. We'll advise you tomorrow morning about our decision. I will walk you down to the foyer and collect the next lady in line."

Abigael looked at Bryan. "Thank you for this opportunity. I hope you find a woman to spend your life with. If it is not me, then I am sure you will find someone perfect. Good luck."

When she returned to find Rosita, she forced herself to listen to the young woman. Her mind kept on returning to the man on the couch. There was something compelling about him. It was as if her soul discovered its other half.

She shook herself as she laughed at her imagination. She often heard of love at first sight, but this was ridiculous. Was this worth moving her whole life to an unknown continent? She never wanted to travel to Africa and even now; it held no great attraction for her. But there was definitely something about Bryan tugging at her heartstrings.

"Abigael, are you okay? You are awfully quiet." Rosita looked at Abigael with worry on her face. "What was this man like? Ugly? Old? A bit crazy?"

"No. He was …. mmmm, surprisingly gorgeous and normal." She blushed as she remembered how her heart beat wildly when he shook her hand.

Peggy and Margaret joined them later in the day and the four women went for a wander down to the beach as the sun set.

"Right ladies, let's compare notes." Abigael suggested. "Peggy, you are first. What did you think of our prospective husband?"

"Well, Carl is dreamy and gorgeous and so sexy I could die. But Bryan, well, he was too quiet for me, really. I like a man who controls the conversation."

"Margaret, did you think the same about Bryan?" Just saying his name brought Abigael into a slight sweat, but she smiled at her compatriots and waited for their reply.

"Bryan looks good, and I checked out how his jeans fit. You can tell a lot about a man by the way he wears his jeans. But no flutters or sparks. Maybe I could learn to like him. It's tough to tell after a fifteen- minute interview." Margaret shook her head.

"He's not my usual type. Too intense, too focused on work. All work and no fun." she said.

"Did Bryan talk much during your interview?" Abigael asked.

"Not a word. He let Carl do all the talking." Margaret admitted.

"But I don't think this job is for me. I like fast cars and to be stuck in the African bush fixing four-wheel-drive vehicles holds no excitement for me. As to the marriage proposal, no, not my idea of fun. I have a boyfriend of sorts back at home. Graham, who wants to marry me and has agreed to let me continue working at the service station in town. In fact, I don't know why I answered the advert at all. Maybe it was to make Graham jealous?" She chuckled to herself for a moment.

Peggy was another matter altogether. She'd imagined life living in a magical romantic setting with her new husband, who seemed much more like Carl than Bryan as she spoke of her dreams. "A big white wedding with wild animals all around us. My man will pick me up and take me to a special home he has built with his own two hands. Oh, I can see it all so clearly."

By the time they returned to the hotel, Abigael knew her two friends would not be her competitors for Bryan and could only hope the other two women would be in a similar mold. They met up with them at the bar. Tilly was right, royally drunk as a skunk. She fell off the bar stool as Abigael tried to prop her upright. "Are you okay Tilly? You seem a little under the weather."

"Yup, weather. Whether I get the job or whether I don't." She quipped. "Do they have coffee in Africa? Can't live without my decaf for breakfast every morning. And wine. Is there wine in the African bush? Lots and lots of wine." Tilly slurred her words badly and it took a moment for the gist of her conversation to make sense.

Her friend, Rebecca, helped her out of the bar and upstairs. Saying over her shoulder, "I don't think the interview went too well for my dear friend Tilly. See you ladies at breakfast. Night, night."

Abigael raised her eyebrows at this display of drunkenness and felt so sad for the young woman. It did not bode well for Tilly and her future as an African bride. Wine or not.

Chapter Three

Sunday morning dawned bright and hot and Bryan knew he couldn't avoid the decision he needed to make. He spread the photos and resumes of the five girls in front of him. Closing his eyes slightly, he tried to remember the impression each woman made on him emotionally.

Peggy spoke to Carl more than him; Margaret spoke non-stop about the Maserati she hoped to buy. Tilly was incredibly sweet and eager to please. Rebecca came across as kind and concerned, but not overly interested in the job. None of these women made a positive impression on Bryan and he now placed the pictures of Rebecca and Abigael on the table in front of him.

Rebecca spent time on a ranch in Texas and seemed sensible and the obvious choice with her extensive understanding of engines and machinery. But Bryan could not get past the look of joy in Abigael's eyes as she helped her fellow competitors. He felt he really needed to get to know them both better before he could make his choice. He called out to Carl, who was just out of the shower and who wandered into the lounge with a towel around his waist.

"I've narrowed it down to two. Rebecca and Abigael. I think we need to take them both to Africa and see how they adjust. We could put them on a three-week trial."

Bryan already made plans in his head to facilitate this new idea. "We can give them both a month to get their affairs in order and then fly them to Johannesburg and go from there. A week in the bush proper and then two weeks taking them around our other projects to gauge their reactions."

"Sure. Anyhow I think you'll choose Rebecca. Abigael will not cut it." Carl stated emphatically.

Bryan frowned at his friend and winked. "We will see."

Walking down to the dining room, they saw the five chosen girls sitting at a table, along with Rosita.

Bryan announced, "Good morning, ladies. We have a decision for you. We feel it is important such a decision should not be rushed, so we have chosen two of you. If you are prepared to join us in Africa for three weeks, we will show you the venues and the projects we are currently working on. This will allow us to get to know each other better. The two we would like to join us are Rebecca and Abigael."

Tilly barely reacted to this decision and the other two girls both smiled as if relieved. Peggy looked at Carl as if she expected him to make a move towards her, but Bryan and Carl spun on their heels and left them to their own devices.

"Carl, I think Peggy has a crush on you, mate?"

Bryan laughed at his friend's blush. "I know, not leggy or dumb enough to make your short list."

After lunch, the women all left for their home journeys and Bryan and Carl spent a few days doing fund raising for Thandi and her latest work project.

Some youngsters in the tribe were digging a dam between two villages and she was eager for a pumping system to allow water to be piped into the homes. This would allow the girls of the tribe to attend school instead of spending their days collecting water from distant rivers. Rivers full of crocodiles and other hazards.

Thandi was in Los Angeles hosting an auction and asked the men to join her in explaining the cost of the work needed. Bryan sourced a painting of an elephant from a well-known wildlife artist who was happy to auction it for the tribe. Carl tapped a few old clients on the shoulders and came up with weekends at holiday resorts and a few spa days for the kitty.

Bryan's parents put up a week's holiday at their home in Zululand for any bovine specialists, of which they hoped there would be a few on the night. Thandi advertised and promoted and been interviewed and spoken on TV shows and finally the time came for the actual auction.

Stephen and Emma Bond arrived from South Africa with photos of their prized Nguni cattle to entice the buyers and at the last moment, found a few artifacts to bring in a few coppers. Intricate bead work and carved wooden animals were mixed in with the more high-end products of the night. Bryan was pleased to meet up with his parents and considered letting them in on his secret of his wife-hunt. But demurred at the last moment. The night was too important to distract his family from what they were trying to achieve. A famous actress agreed to run the auction and the press was out in force as the crowds gathered.

Thandi stood at the door with Carl and Bryan, dressed in their best versions of smart chic they could manage. Thandi herself was dressed in an African print dress. A marvel of well-fitted exotic elegance. Cameras flashed from the waiting press and Thandi reminded the men to smile sweetly.

She placed a hand on Bryan's arm as they stood together and whispered, "How did it go with the prospective brides?"

"We narrowed it down to two potential candidates. Carl and I will bring them both to South Africa for an orientation tour. You will get to meet them and hopefully help me choose." Bryan whispered back as the mayor of the city mounted the steps.

The rest of the evening went off without a hitch and, after expenses, they were pleased to note the dollar signs in the ledger.

"This should be enough for two pumps at least." Thandi did the quick mental calculations. "I could make a second dam and with a little bit more fundraising, I could pay you guys for your hard work."

Bryan loosened his tie and sat back in his chair, satisfied with the proceeds of the evening. The person who won the trip to visit his parent's farm in Zululand was a Texan rancher and extremely excited about seeing this uniquely African bovine. The wildlife painting reached top dollar and was now being carried out the door by a very pleased art critic and collector. Now Bryan could turn his attention to his friends and family.

He smiled at Thandi as she scrolled through the hydraulic pumps on offer. She put her laptop out on the table and flicked through different options. Bryan was happy to let her dream of clean, pure water and imagine her tribe's benefit health wise as well as educating the youngsters. He should speak to her about building a school while they were working in the area. But not tonight. Tonight, was to celebrate the conclusion of a successful auction.

Stephen clapped his hand on his son's shoulder. "I read somewhere you are looking for a wife who can do a bit of engineering work on the side?"

The shock was clear on Bryan's face as he looked at Carl and Thandi, who were both avoiding his eyes assiduously. And then he turned to see how his mother handled the information.

Emma smiled through the tears in her eyes as she said, "I want you to be happy, son. Your lack of a partner who can encourage you and work by your side has been in my prayers for years. I hope this endeavour has a good outcome. And I am so proud of you for thinking of more than just looks and sex appeal."

Bryan blushed and laughed with his mother. "I have found two ladies who might fit the bill. They will be in South Africa in a few weeks' time. I might bring them to the farm to meet you all." There really was no way to keep secrets in his family. And it felt good knowing his parents approved in principle.

Chapter Four

Abigael was having a harder time keeping her family happy with her decision. Her mother ranted and raved. Her father shook his head and mumbled about an ungrateful child being like a serpent. But it was Grandma who really brought out all the emotional blackmail tools in her kit.

"I lived through the death camps and the ghettos and barely survived. But this will kill me. You are murdering an old woman with your heartless choices. Running away to sleep with a stranger. At least tell me he's a good Jewish man. And what are you going to eat? Kosher? You are throwing away the hard work of all your ancestors to chase a dream. Don't talk to me."

She sobbed as Abigael tried to give her a hug. "You are dead to me. I'm glad your grandfather is gone; this would have broken his heart." She threw her arms up in the air and stumbled down the passage towards her rooms.

Only Joe seemed happy with this turn of events. "I always knew you wouldn't be able to find a husband without becoming nothing more than a prostitute. He is buying your honor and body with blood money. How do you know he is not a slave owner?"

"Oh Joe, stop living in the ancient past. There is no chance of him being a slave owner. And anyway, I am used to slavery. It's what I have been to this family." Abigael snapped.

"Oh vey. Oh vey. You are a wicked daughter, Abigael. You are not the joy of your father. You are the heartbreak. Maybe we should change your name?" Her mother wailed as she, too, walked out of the room.

This left only her father and Joe to stare at her in anger. "When do you go?" was all her father said as she sat with shaking hands and a heavy heart.

"Three weeks' time Dad. I can hand over my job at the firm to Joe and make sure he is aware of all the projects we have planned. And if he can't find someone to help, well, I am sure they have the internet in Africa. I could send you the online manual for my latest job and Rachel can do the diagrams like she normally does anyway."

"There is no reason I must be in the office to do the work. I can do it as well as if I sat at a desk across from you." Abigael tried to appease her father and brother as she continued to sit at the kitchen table.

"It won't be the same. You have always been there to check Rachel doesn't connect the wrong pipe to the incorrect outlet tube. My eyes are dim. There is no way I can do it." Abe Rabinowitz said sadly.

"Well, don't look at me to fix the problem, Dad. I don't know one end of an engine to another. I'm purely a manager. I thought Abi would be here till she retired and not leaving us in the lurch like this. This is pretty inconsiderate of you, sis." Joe admitted.

They spoke through the ramifications for an hour and then all went off to bed. Abigael couldn't sleep as she tossed and turned. Was she a viper? A traitor to the family? She finally got up and looked at the photo of her beloved grandfather and spoke to him.

"Zeyde, what should I do? What would you tell me to do?"

But there were no straightforward answers and finally Abigael fell asleep just as the sun rose. As sleep overtook her, she imagined sitting on her grandfather's knee and him patting her on the head.

A voice she knew and loved whispered into her dreams. "Live life to the fullest, my dearest kind. Grasp the future and live."

She smiled at those oft repeated admonishments.

"Yes Zeyde, I will, I will." She whispered into her pillow and allowed the demons of the night to dissipate.

The following few weeks were filled with catching up on projects and organising her assistant to take over new ones. Herman was pleased to get this promotion to senior technical writer and walked around like a puffed-up pigeon, lording it over the other workers until Abigael told him to behave. At no time did she ever say this move might not be permanent. She allowed her family and co-workers to assume this was to be her future. A lifetime of romance and love in the wilds of Africa. There were a few young women who got all starry-eyed at the idea and Abigael laughed at their comments of "you are so lucky" and "I wish it was me."

Rachel and Sara took her out to lunch and grilled her on what her future husband was like. Abigael smiled as she remembered each feature of his face and figure and her sisters were convinced it would become a love match to beat all love matches their shadchan, the marriage broker, could arrange.

"All those silly boys the woman set you up with were no match for you. You have brains and are the nicest person I know, sorry Sara." Rachel said.

"Oh, I agree dear sister. She is certainly nicer than you." Sara responded with a grin.

"Well, this man better realise you are a gem, Abigael. Remember some men are diamonds and others are stones. And the difference is often in how they treat you. But then, you need to sometimes put the man under a bit of pressure and heat to change him into a diamond. Lots of heat." Rachel added with a smirk.

"Oh, heck yeah. Without heat in the marriage, you might as well be dead. No fun without some naughty fun." Sara and Rachel put their arms around their sister in affection as they walked out of the restaurant.

They insisted on buying her racy and scandalous underwear making Abigael blush to the roots of her hair. Her two sisters dragged her into an upmarket lingerie shop with prices to shock and designs to delight.

"Undies from Heaven and prices from hell," Sara whispered to Abigael as they looked at the offerings.

Choosing a dozen lacy and silky outfits for Abigael and a few for themselves, Abigael was pleased it was not her footing the bill.

And then came the sex talk. To say there were interesting ideas of what a Jewish woman could do and what she was not, was, to put it mildly, scandalous.

"Remember Abi Jewish women do not go to heaven, and we need to make this life as pleasurable as possible for ourselves. If your husband does not fulfill all your sexual and emotional needs, then get busy girl. Do not sit back and wait for miracles. Tell him exactly what floats your boat and tell him to get with the plan." Sara insisted.

"Oh heck, yes. And sex toys. Well, they were made for a reason. I have a drawer full of fun things." Rachel admitted. "The only problem is the kids are nosy and last month Avram came into the lounge holding a sex toy out to our guests, offering it as a gift. My husband nearly died of embarrassment." She hooted with laughter at the memory. "Six years old and already I have to hide things from him at the top of my cupboard."

Things only got raunchier as they took her into a male strip club for an educational tour. Their oldest sister, Zlota, joined them. As she sat down with a handful of dollar bills clutched in her hand, she said, "So have you filled in Abi about married life?"

"Of course. She is not going into this adventure without us telling her all she needs to know." Rachel said.

"Yeah, right, I know you two women. You would have told her all the things you enjoy and not told her the most important part of sex and love," Zlota replied defiantly.

"Well, what would you tell her if you were so experienced?" Sara added.

"Communication. Talk to the man. Tell him when you are happy and what makes you sad. Men are not mind readers. They like things spelled out for them. Oh, and please, do not use sex as a punishment."

Zlota shook her head. "You are only making your own life a misery. What if you don't enjoy performing for your man when he wants it? Well, suck it up, girlie. Say yes and you never know it might be the best sex you have ever experienced."

Looking over at her two sisters, she shook her finger at them. "And you could learn a lesson, too. If you treat your husband like a king and expect him to treat you like a queen, well, life is much happier. Trust me."

And it was true Zlota was the happiest of the three married sisters. Her husband Aaron and she often hugged and kissed in public, much to the disgust of their children.

Abigael tried to insist she return to work at some stage, but her three sisters shouted her down and told her life was for living. Their grandfather told them each they should grasp the opportunities in life.

This argument silenced all Abigael's objections, and she allowed her sisters to dictate what else they should do. The strip club was followed by a dance club and somewhere around midnight they ended up at a diner eating burgers and fries washed down with hot coffee to sober them up.

Abigael did not drink as much as her sisters, but she felt lightheaded as they caught taxis to their respective homes. She would miss their company in Africa and a lump rose in her throat as she bid them goodnight.

On the morning of her departure, Rachel's husband came into her office and sat down. Nigel was the only non-Jew in the family and was arguably the only thing Rachel ever did wrong in her parent's eyes. But Abigael loved her brother-in-law.

He was such a lovely man. When he married her sister, she felt a twinge of regret he didn't find her first. The moment he saw Rachel, he was smitten and never looked at another woman since.

"Abi, tell me the truth. Is this a done deal? Are you really going to marry a stranger?" Nigel asked in a concerned way.

"Nigel, love can grow, and I think Bryan and I can work together to make each other happy. If things don't work out, it won't be the end of the world. I can always come home." Abigael winced at the thought.

"Oh no, Abi. Don't. If things turn to custard, travel and see the world. Don't come back." He smiled. "I love working with you and your company, but I hate to see the way the men in this family treat you. You are better than this. Don't trade one poor relationship for another. Call me if you need help." Nigel stood up, ready to leave.

"I know how much we have paid you over the years Abi, and you are worth much more. Take your savings and live life to the fullest. Live the dream for those of us who cannot get out of the rat race."

What was it with people telling her to live life to the full? Packing up the last of her things from her desk, she looked up to see all the staff assembled in the main office. Judy, the office manager, produced an enormous cake with Bon voyage emblazoned across it. Nigel revealed a bulky parcel, resembling a set of luggage. And even Joe was there to make a speech and wish her luck. Toasts were drunk and women cried and hugged. The men patted her shoulder and wished her a good life and Nigel loaded her into a taxi and waved her goodbye.

When she got home, her parents and grandmother stood at the curb waiting for her. "Come here, my child. Let me hug you one last time." Her grandmother called.

Abigael struggled to extricate herself from the cab as her grandmother stood weeping on the kerb.

Her mother and grandmother even helped her pack her extra bags and finally Abe accompanied her to the airport and cried as she walked away to start her new life.

"Come home if you are not happy. All will be forgiven." her father begged.

But all it did was make her more determined to make it work in Africa. She did nothing to be forgiven for. Nothing to be ashamed of. And her father's words set her teeth on edge as she struggled to keep her anger at bay.

It was only as the plane lifted off and New York shrunk into the darkness below her, that the finality of her decision hit Abigael.

She cried as there was no going back for her. Nigel was right, and she felt Zeyde's spirit with her as she relaxed at last. All she could do was hope a better life awaited her at the other end of the flight. Her seat was at a window and she was soon chatting to the old grandmother sitting next to her.

"Oh, how romantic. A mail order bride." the old lady said. "When I married my husband, it was the Hippy era and my friends told me to live with him first. But I suppose I am old fashioned. And we were very happy for the forty years we remained married." She sighed. "Well, I was happy. But at his funeral I found out there were other women in his life. One woman in particular acted like she was the real widow and wailed like a cat being murdered."

She nodded her head. "Stan, my husband, left me well off and I am taking advantage of every penny. I have a safari planned in the Serengeti and then a few weeks in Paris. I might even go to Egypt for a cruise up the Nile. I made one mistake in my marriage." She admitted. "I believed his lies."

Soon the old lady tired of their conversation and nodded off to sleep. Abigael read a novel for a few hours and then she too joined her seating companion in a snooze.

Sixteen hours later, they landed in a world as different as it could be from New York as was possible. Carl and Bryan waited for her to disembark, and it was Carl who was the first to give her a welcome hug as Bryan took control of the bags. The noise and the smells were so overpowering, it took her a few moments to realise Bryan was talking to her.

"Did you have a pleasant flight? Not too tired, I hope?" The pleasantries continued as they walked through the concourse and towards the parking garage.

She saw the old grandmother waving from the taxi rank and blew her a kiss. "Enjoy your safari." She called out.

Abigael looked around at the vendors swarming around and the glimpses of heat distorted hills in the distance as Bryan guided her to a parking area.

The air-conditioned luxury vehicle was a pleasant surprise as they drove down the highway. "We are meeting up with Rebecca tomorrow morning. For tonight, we are at the Sun City hotel and will go through some orientation stuff when you are well rested." Bryan informed her.

He sat in the front seat alongside Carl and turned around to speak to her over his headrest. Not sure what to say to this virtual stranger, Abigael smiled and leaned back in the seat. She peered out the window as Bryan pointed out the mine dumps left over from a century of gold mines apparently forming a network of tunnels right under the city. Almost three hours later, they reached their destination. By this time, Abigael succumbed to sleep and was woken up by a nudge to the shoulder.

"Come on sleepy head, you have reached the hotel. I will show you your rooms and order you some food. Don't worry, I am not expecting you to be the life and soul of the party tonight. Sleep for a few hours and we will meet up again tomorrow." Bryan commented.

He helped Abigael gently out of the seat, and they walked past an impressive foyer, where he picked up a key to her cabana. Leading her down a passageway, they reached a suite with a view of a sparkling pool and green lawns dappled with the shade of large trees.

Abigael said "Thank you, Bryan. I will be more aware of things once I have snoozed and maybe scrubbed off this jet lag in a nice hot shower?"

He leaned forward and kissed her on the cheek. His hot breath caressing her cheek softly. "Sure Abi. I have ordered you a piece of salmon and a salad, followed by apple pie and ice-cream for dinner. I will see you tomorrow. I am staying in the cabana next door, so knock if there is anything you need from me."

True to his word, a delicious meal was delivered, and it surprised Abigael to know she was so hungry. She took a photo of her meal and her surroundings and sent it off to her family to tell them she arrived safely. But the shower and her bed beckoned her.

Her eyes felt like there was sandpaper in them and she was eager to close them. Soft towels and a robe in the shower area awaited her and she was ready for bed, full and clean and happy. Touching her cheek where Bryan's kiss lingered, and she smiled as sleep overtook her.

Chapter Five

Rebecca arrived during the night and was bright and chirpy at breakfast. "Abi, they bumped me up to first class on the flight. I told the steward I was a mail-order bride for a great white hunter in Africa and they were so impressed they treated me like a queen. The chair was so comfortable. It reclined right down, and I got all the sleep I needed on the flight over. Isn't this hotel amazing?"

Carl and Bryan wandered into the dining area and joined them at their table. "How do you like your accommodation? Sadly, it will only be for another night and then we need to get on the road." Carl, as usual, was the spokesperson for the duo and smiled happily at the looks on the girls' faces. "Today we are going on a wildlife drive so you can see the animals which have made this place famous."

Bryan looked over at Abigael to watch her smile at him with her bright face beaming. "This is spectacular, Bryan. This is more than I ever imagined I would find in Africa."

"Ah, now, don't get too complacent about Africa. This place is geared towards tourists and in no way reflects the rest of the area." Bryan admitted as he glanced around at the theatrical looking dining room with its oversized carvings of elephants adorning the gates.

Rebecca wore a sundress as short as it could get, and Bryan frowned at the idea of her climbing into the viewing vehicle flashing legs for all and sundry. Carl would be happy to take in the view, but Bryan knew he would not be swayed by the sight of a slim leg or two. He saw his fair share of legs in his time. He was not averse to the view, but this was serious business for him.

Abigael wore a pair of shorts and a shirt, along with a pair of strappy sandals highlighting her honey-colored skin. Who was he fooling? He was distracted and would be even if they wore full length dresses and long sleeves? Both the women had their own special attraction and Bryan knew the choice was a difficult one if all he looked at were their bodies.

Carl helped the women up from their chairs and Bryan joined them as they went to find their sightseeing guide.

Thomas, the guide, was a Zulu man with a big grin and a patter well-rehearsed and slick. "We go to play with lion cubs first, ladies. You men can join us, of course, but be aware it is the women who love the kitties the most." He laughed.

And so, it was. Rebecca took a dozen photos of herself cuddling cubs to send to her family. And Abigael asked questions about why they were so tame, and they would ever be set free.

"Are cubs used as a tourist attraction, Thomas? Surely this is not their natural environment?" Abigael queried.

Bryan stood back and observed quietly as Thomas obliged with answers. Although Abigael enjoyed having the cubs playing around her, it was the Springbok she was most impressed with. Touching Bryan's arm as she noticed the baby buck hiding behind its mother's flank, she leaned into him and whispered, "They are so amazing. And I am so glad these are wild and not having to be pawed by tourist's day and night."

A warm glow spread through his body at her touch, and he put his arm around her shoulder as he turned her towards where a giraffe and its baby could be seen in the bushland. "It's the season for babies. Look at how protective the mother giraffe is?"

Her reaction was so genuine he wanted to show her more. Thomas pointed to a rhino and then the sighting of the day as a family of warthogs ran across the road with their tails up in the air.

Bryan saw Rebecca staring at the two of them and their closeness. "Bry, could you tell me a bit about the wildlife in the area you live?" She batted her eyelashes at him. A small pink tongue came out and licked her lips as she waited for his answer.

"Oh, dear Rebecca, are you thirsty? Don't let your lips get dry. Thomas, do we have any more chilled water for the ladies?" Bryan asked.

He did not like anyone shortening his name and her calling him Bry irritated him slightly. He looked over at Carl to see his old friend laughing softly at the situation.

"Yes, Bry, tell us all you know about African wildlife. Why don't you?" Carl teased.

"I would not presume to tell you about the wild animals. After all, it is what we are paying Thomas for." He growled at Carl, who winked at him in reply.

And Thomas did inform them. He gave them facts and figures and funny stories non-stop during the rest of their day. They stopped alongside a small dam for lunch and, true to form, the hotel supplied an impressive picnic for them to enjoy.

Monkeys played in the trees and bright yellow birds wove nests hanging from the branches. Bryan pointed out the way the female bird inspected the nests the males created. "The narrow entry always points downwards." Bryan informed them.

"Oh yes, it's to stop those pesky snakes from eating the eggs and chicks." Thomas announced. "Naughty snakes who would never deign to scare you ladies." He laughed.

"Thomas, you are a very good liar." Abigael admitted. And Thomas shrugged his shoulders in admittance of guilt.

Rebecca turned to Bryan and said "You will protect me from snakes, won't you Bry?"

"I will certainly try." Bryan said with a blush.

After lunch, they visited an African village with amazingly decorated homes. Homes painted with geometric patterns in a variety of earth tones. "The women of the tribe do the decorating and seldom use paintbrushes." Bryan informed them.

They were taken inside by the guides and could buy some of the beadwork and carvings. Both Abigael and Rebecca bought them for their families back home.

Bryan was careful to spend equal time with each woman and with a woman on both arms as they wandered through the village. He noticed Rebecca kept on grabbing his hand and wanting him to focus on her most of the time. Abigael was totally different and was happy to chat to the lady at the shop about the possibility of exporting some of her work to New York.

"My sister has a fashion house and some of these belts are so different from what you can buy over there. Do you mind if I send her some photos of your work? And do you have a business card I could send her?" Abigael asked.

Ntombi, the saleslady, was quick to supply the card and happily pose alongside the belts and bags.

As they climbed into the vehicle to return to the hotel, Rebecca leaned over and said to Bryan. "I noticed a lot of the youngsters have no shoes. I thought I could get some of my friends to do a shoe drive in the States and we could parcel them up and send them out here to help?"

Bryan took a deep breath as he decided how to tell her tactfully her help was not wanted or needed. "Rebecca, if you send European shoes out here to Africa, it means a local shoemaker loses his job. If the shoemaker loses his job, he cannot teach the next generation his skills. It would be better if you did not send shoes to these people. My brother-in-law always says we need to give the poor a hand up and not a handout. Giving them things. We feel they need means they become dependent on us. All it does is stroke our own egos. These youngsters are happy with no shoes. If they really wanted shoes, they would find a way of making their own or buying them."

The look of shock and horror on Rebecca's face was a surprise. "There is no need to be mean to me, Bry. I was only trying to be kind to these people."

"Yes, Rebecca. And I appreciate it is your generosity causing you to make this offer. But really, they are a proud people and being given stuff demeans them." Bryan smiled as he helped her understand his viewpoint.

"Oh Bry, you are so sweet. Of course, you didn't mean to be nasty. I am so sensitive to people who have less of the luxuries in life and want to help where I can."

Over her shoulder, Bryan could see Carl pulling a face at him at this conversation and its outcome. "Right, time to get back and have a swim on the lovely beach. Come along Thomas, chop, chop." Bryan suggested.

When they got to their cabana, Carl whispered to Bryan. "I'm seriously re-considering my choice for your wife. She is clueless. I think she has a Santa Claus fetish and wants to hand out goodies. Or maybe she thinks Africa needs a white Saviour? Mmm, not sure it will go down well with the folk we work with?"

Bryan scowled at his friend. "Yup, but she didn't know any better and maybe now she will see things differently."

But at heart Bryan realised living with Rebecca would not be ideal. In fact, he was already hoping she would return home to the States before the three-week trial was up. Three weeks of her flirting and girlishness would drive him insane.

But she looked good in a bikini. And she swam like a fish in the engineered waves on the transplanted fake beach. Abigael wore a simple one piece not doing much to enhance her slim figure, rounded hips and ample bosom. He saw Carl eyeing the two women and was not surprised to hear him say.

"Abigael has short legs. Nice bum, but those legs should have been longer. Now, Rebecca, she looks more appealing the more of her I see."

Smacking his friend on the arm, Bryan ran into the waves and floated on his back, enjoying the gentle movement of the water. He could hear through the water the laughter of those around him. He raised his head to see Abigael swimming in the waves with a huge smile on her face.

"This is luxury. I'm not sure my sisters would believe me if I told them this whole thing is engineered?" Her smile was contagious and Bryan knew he was grinning like a silly boy.

Rebecca and Carl strolled along the shallow waves at the edge and seemed to have an in-depth conversation. For a moment, he wondered what they were talking about. But then the soothing waters washed all his cares away. He did not realise how stressful this balancing act of having two women after his attention would be. Taking a deep breath, he wondered if three weeks would be too much for his peace of mind?

Bryan swam up next to Abigael and joined her body surfing fun. The water was so clear he could watch the play of sunlight on the sandy bottom of the pool as they rode the waves. Finally, as if by common agreement, they both ended their swims and returned to the others.

"Wow, the best fun ever." Abigael admitted. "I can tick off my bucket list, swimming in an inland sea. If there was a bucket list. And if I'd even known such a thing existed." she laughed shaking off the sea sand from her feet before slipping them into her sandals.

Bryan noted her toenails were not painted and he smiled. Who knew toenails could be sexy, he thought.

Dinner was a juggling act to keep Rebecca happy while not neglecting Abigael. They went to a live show, and it was a strange feeling to have the hands of the two women on either side gripping him.

Rebecca's icy hands with long slim fingers wove themselves between his. Abigael's hands were smaller, and he loved the feeling of his hand engulfing hers. What the show was all about, he could not remember. He knew it was a famous comedienne followed by an almost as famous singer. But there was no recollection of the jokes told or the songs sung. He spent the evening weighing up the pros and cons of each woman. And by the end, he knew who he wanted to marry.

Bryan walked the women to their rooms and kissed them each on the cheek. Rebecca threw her arms around his neck and whispered. "Thank you for a wonderful day. If all our days in Africa are like this, I will be happy to stay." She blushed prettily and smiled.

Abigael looked him in the eyes. "Sleep well Bryan, you look tired out." Before turning around and waving over her shoulder at him.

Why is it he found the wave far more erotic than the hug and kiss? Carl patted him on the back. "Time for a bit of reflection, mate. Who is pushing your libido buttons, hey?"

He laughed as he turned to his own room. "Sweet dreams and keep them clean, Bry. No saucy stuff just yet."

Sleep came easily as thoughts of Abigael floated through his mind. Now the decision was made, he could play the kind host to Rebecca and let her down as kindly as he could. An owl hooted outside his window, and he sighed, already half asleep.

The following morning, they climbed into their car and started driving South. Carl took the wheel and Bryan asked Rebecca if she would like to sit up front to get the best views of the countryside. "We will swap around later in the day. It's an eight-hour journey, so there will be plenty of time for us all to have a turn in the front."

They skirted the city of Pretoria with its traffic and crime issues and drove down the highway at speed. They stopped at Ermelo for lunch at a quaint restaurant called the Makou and Bryan was happy to see Abigael tucking into a large plate of food, while Rebecca picked at a salad. Abigael didn't ask if it was Kosher, and Bryan felt relieved when he made a query on her behalf and was told all their meals were Kosher and Halal.

He settled down in the seat between the women and said to Abigael. "The chef says it is Kosher, in case you wanted to know."

Rebecca stopped eating her crispy bacon on lettuce and apple. "Why do you need Kosher? You are not Jewish, are you?"

"Yup, born and bred." Abigael said with a smile. "With a name like mine, I am surprised everyone didn't already know?"

"What is your name? I only know you as Abi. Does it have some religious significance or something?" Rebecca asked.

"Well, it was the name of one of King David's wives in the Christian bible and in our Tanakh. Which is like your Old Testament." Seeing Rebecca was still no closer to understanding the relevance.

"My name means a father's joy in Yiddish. And my surname is Rabinowitz, which is a well-known surname amongst Jews." She shrugged her shoulders at a still baffled Rebecca.

"In fact, your own name is derived from the scriptures. Rebecca was the wife of Jacob and means to tie or bind up someone." She smiled at Rebecca and Bryan was pleased to see there was no animosity in her look.

"I have three sisters, Zlota, which is Yiddish for a gold coin. Rachel, who was the favorite wife of Jacob. And the youngest is Sara, who in the scriptures was the wife of Abraham and means a princess or someone of high rank." She waited for Rebecca to reply to her information, but all she got was a confused look.

The whole way through lunch, Rebecca said hardly one word and for a moment Bryan was concerned about her. But then she grabbed his hand under the table, and he knew she was processing what she heard, and she was fine.

Rebecca sat at the back with Carl after lunch and they continued on to the highway. Suddenly Bryan wanted to share his love for the country with Abigael and began a tour guide style discourse.

"The Kruger Park is to the North of us and is as big as a European country all on its own. The Great Rift Valley starts in the Eritrea peninsula stretches through the continent of Africa and ends up in Mocambique, which is to our left. Then there is the kingdom of Swaziland and finally we are about to enter my home county of KwaZulu. This is where we are working at the moment. Our boss is Thandi Gumede, the tribal leader of a group of Zulus."

He knew he overdid the monologue and took a moment to glance over at Abigael to see how she took his sudden talkativeness. But there was no sign of boredom. He could hear Carl softly snoring in the back seat after his large lunch, but Abigael was bright eyed and obviously interested in all he was saying. A quick look in his rearview mirror told him Rebecca was on her cell phone and showing no fascination with these insights.

The hours sped by as Abigael asked Bryan about the cultivation, she could see out her window. Rows and rows of pineapples. She admitted she was clueless about how pineapples grew and when they came across a roadside stall; they stopped to buy a few bags of fruit from the vendor.

Abigael snacked on juicy guavas and tried a marula, and a mango, salivating at the exotic taste. "Nice. I could live on fruit Bryan. This is so fresh and nothing like what we get in New York." He leaned forward and wiped a drop of juice off her chin. Licking his finger and winking at her as she grinned in reply.

Rebecca sighed and said "But do you know what fertilizer they use and are they genetically pure?"

"Oh yeah. Totally natural. These people farm in the ancient ways, Rebecca. No fancy tricks, just pure nature at its best." Bryan said with a grin.

They were staying the night at another hotel, the Ghost Mountain Inn, in the shadow of the Lebombo mountain range and its iconic Ghost Mountain. Built in 1962 when the family found people were in need of accommodation, and there were no other hotels in the area. The Rutherford family decided to build.

"I came here many years ago with my parents." Bryan admitted. "It's changed a bit since then, but it is still as friendly as it ever was."

As they drove into the car park, Abigael leaned forward. "Why the strange name? Are there really ghosts?"

"Well, no, not at the hotel. But the locals say you can see the lights of the dead kings as they walk towards the Ghost Mountain on particular moonless nights. I have never seen them." He laughed, "Maybe tonight we will be lucky?"

"Well, I am not in the least bit interested in ghosts. Near or far." Rebecca announced from the back seat. "Oh goodie, I see they have a spa here. Well, I know what I am doing this evening. A relaxing massage is my idea of heaven."

The car barely stopped in front of the foyer before a uniformed concierge jumped forward to open their doors and assist them out of the vehicle.

"Ah, Bryan Bond. It is good to have you visit once more. You are always welcome. And you too Carl Young. And two lovely ladies, what a pleasure" He shook all their hands and unloaded their luggage onto a trolley. Speaking all the while, he led them inside towards the desk, where he handed them over to an effusive receptionist. She booked a massage and a body scrub for Rebecca and then turned to Abigael to ask if she, too, would enjoy a spa visit.

"No, thank you. I plan to sit and watch the sunset at the pool and maybe have a glass of ice-cold fruit juice before dinner. But, no, I am quite relaxed, thanks."

Bryan and Carl agreed to join her at the pool after settling into their rooms. Rebecca waved over her shoulder as she followed the signs to the spa. Bryan was happy to see the back of her and glad to relax for a moment. No doubt she would join them for dinner, but until then, he could enjoy the peace and quiet.

Chapter Six

Abigael considered wearing her one-piece swimming costume again, but the sight of the cheeky bikini her sisters bought her tempted her. Putting a sarong around herself to hide her wide hips and her extra wobbly bits as much as she could, she wandered down to the pool. As she approached the two men, they turned, and Carl gave a wolf whistle.

"Oh, so much better than what you wore yesterday. Much better."

Abigael blushed crimson. She'd never been whistled at before. Not even the construction workers in New York considered her worth their whistling efforts. The high sides of the bikini did something to her legs to make them look slightly longer and she was grateful for her sister's fashion sense. The bottom half was a deep blue and the top a slightly lighter blue with the same tiny dots all over it and the sarong was just the perfect length to skim over her hips and hide the things she hated most about her body.

Bryan rose from his seat and towered over her as he helped her into a lounger. "What do you want to drink, Abigael?" He asked with a husky voice.

Clearing his throat slightly, he said, "Pineapple juice or guava? They are both excellent."

As they waited for the server to bring their drinks, Abigael said to Carl.

"Do you know I have never been given a wolf whistle in my life? You were my first. I am a wolf whistle virgin." She laughed.

"And it is no wonder if you cover up like you have done before. Now, if you walked down a New York Street dressed in a bikini, I know you would cause at least one traffic accident, I can assure you." Carl commented as he eyed her up and down.

"I like leggy blondes, but seriously, girl, you need to show your figure off a bit more."

Bryan cleared his throat once more and frowned at his friend. "What do you think, Bryan? Do you think I should dress like this more often?" Abigael asked.

"I think you look beautiful no matter what you wear, Abigael. Your beauty shines out of your eyes and your love of life is infectious. You don't need to dress like this all the time, but now and again, well, it is a sight for sore eyes. You are stunning."

"Well, thank you, kind sirs. You have made this girl's day."

When Rebecca joined them an hour later, Abigael was surprised neither man whistled at her. She, too, changed into a bikini and with a wraparound skirt swinging from her hips in a swirl of colour.

She wore high heels making Abigael feel diminutive as they walked into the dining room to collect a meal they would eat under the stars around the pool. But somehow, she was not intimidated by this confident and beautiful woman who was her competitor in this duel of the dames.

The hour she spent with Carl and Bryan helped her feel comfortable in her own skin. They listened to her as she spoke about her excitement at seeing Africa through their eyes. She felt accepted and happy in their company.

"I can see the poverty in the rural areas, but oh my dear, the scenery is divine. I have grown up in New York where our skyline is cluttered with buildings, and here, well, it is as if the world has expanded from horizon to horizon and beyond." Abigael gushed.

Rebecca smiled at her. "Girl, visit me in Texas sometime. When you sit on your horse on the ridge, well, the horizon vanishes into the distance, and it feels like the heavens are touching the earth."

This was the first time Rebecca ever spoke directly to Abigael about her life, and she was pleased. Abigael hated the thought of not being friends with her fellow American.

"Thanks Rebecca. I would love to visit. Not sure about riding horses, though. I took some lessons when I was a young girl, and the family visited a guest ranch one Summer."

The two men sat and watched the two women get to know each other and talked quietly about the days ahead. Tomorrow morning, they were driving to Maputo land and onto the Makatini flats where Thandi would wait for them. They needed a four-wheel-drive vehicle and would leave their upmarket car behind in a secure garage in Mkuze township. The roads were less than inviting and both men worried the women might find it tough going.

Over time, they became accustomed to the rattle and roll of the corrugated roads, but for a first timer, it was confronting. The wet season was over for a few months and at least the roads were not bogged down with mud. But they were dusty, and Carl knew from experience they would have to keep the windows wound up to breathe and the heat inside the cab could be horrendous. Storms rampaged across the countryside most summer afternoons and if they timed it right, they could reach their destination before they hit.

Bryan whispered, "We might need to buy some handheld, battery operated fans for the ladies."

"Sure, sounds like a good idea." Carl admitted as Bryan turned to smile at the females.

"Are you ready for a swim?" The moon was high overhead and the total area looked like a fairyland under the sparkle of the heavens. Bryan asked.

Taking each woman by a hand, he pulled them upright and then, before they could refuse, he ran into the tepid water. Carl did a bomb, swamping them with a deluge of water. They all enjoyed the pool as they played around in the water. It might not be as elaborate as the engineered, man-made sea they enjoyed the night before, but it was perfect at the end of the long drive.

Bryan found a ball and threw it into the pool. A few other guests joined them, and they started a game of water polo between the groups of tourists. Laughter and giggles ensued as people jumped and hit the ball between the loosely assembled teams. Rules were totally forgotten as they focused on fun. At the end of the evening, Bryan heard one youngster say it was the most fun so far on this African wildlife tour.

Both women joined in wholeheartedly and he watched Abigael interact with the children in the pool. She was a natural and didn't speak down to them at all. Chatting to them as if they were interesting. Listening to what they said and not talking over them condescendingly.

"Yes, Simon, school can be a pain, but if you think of your goals, it's worth all the hard work. You can be anything you wish. You have the world at your feet. Find what makes you happy. I did. And now I tinker with engines and write about it all day. I love my job." She said to the teenager who five minutes before was pouting and angry with life.

Simon's father almost undid all the good work Abigael did when he yelled out. "Come here, you lazy, good for nothing. Get your father another beer."

Simon rolled his eyes and Abigael smiled at Bryan over his head before saying, "If you don't study, you might end up serving obnoxious men beers in some pub. Study and rise to your potential." She patted his arm and Simon's smile said it all.

Abigael walked over to Bryan and laughed. "Too much preachy, preachy Bryan? I promise I am not trying to be the big white saviour of Africa."

He put his arm around her shoulders and pulled her closer for a hug. Kissing the top of her head, he said, "Nope, not too preachy, preachy. Just pretty gorgeous is what you are."

"Aah Bryan, you told me I was gorgeous before. Are you sure you don't need glasses? Or suffer from myopia?" She teased.

"I have twenty-twenty vision, I promise you. And yes, I think you are gorgeous."

He looked up to see Rebecca glaring at him from the pool and smiled at her. "Time to get to bed, Rebecca. It's a big day tomorrow. You need to be rested when we take on the dreaded Makatini roading system."

Chapter Seven

Bryan and Carl escorted the women to their rooms and bid them goodnight.

Abigael and Rebecca stood watching as they walked away into the darkness. "What do you think tomorrow will be like?" Rebecca asked quietly into the gloom.

"I rather think this is where we leave civilisation, Rebecca. I did a sneaky look at a map of the area and there seem to be lots of game reserves and not much in the way of towns and definitely no cities around here. I only hope I can handle this life. I have never lived further than five minutes from a mall or at least a shop of some sort."

"Yes, me too. Well, a little bit further than five minutes, actually. But I get the idea we need to make sure we have everything we need before we go any further." Rebecca admitted.

Turning to Abigael, she looked at her competitor. "Not to be rude, Abi. But I don't think you stand a chance against me. First, you are Jewish. And second, you have never lived in the wilds. I think I will be the one he chooses. I am sorry. If you want to leave now, tell them before we go bush. I think Bryan would appreciate a bit of honesty."

Abigael felt her mouth open in surprise as she gaped at Rebecca. "No, I am not giving up so easily, Rebecca. And even if Bryan chooses you, well, I have to at least give it my best."

"Sure, sweetie but look at you. If we stood in front of a mirror, who would you choose as the winner?" She did a quick twirl, and showing off her svelte figure. There were no noticeable bulges or flabby bits at all. She was muscle and slim lines, and Abigael knew if they were being chosen by looks alone, then she would be the loser.

"Well, we shall see." Abigael wanted to say at least the men whistled at her and her sister, Zlota always reminded her men did not look at bodies as women did. All her life she compared herself to other, more beautiful women, and it took all her courage to pretend what Rebecca said did not hurt her.

Entering her hotel room, she was drawn to the mirror in the bathroom, and she stood staring at herself for a moment. After the evening's activity in the pool, her hair was a mess and there was no hint of make-up on her face.

Turning her back to the mirror, she leaned over her shoulder and stared at her rear end. Well-rounded is what her mother called it. Her hips formed a small platform she could rest her hands on. Not ideal model material but was it what she yearned for? Absolutely, Abigael admitted to herself. A model figure would be the cherry on the top.

She compared herself to girls she grew up with, and none of them looked anything like her. Tears gathered in the corners of her eyes as she turned around once more to look critically at her body.

It was with a heavy heart she climbed into bed and thought of her grandfather. What advice would he give her? What would he think of her crying into her pillow when outside her window was the stunning beauty of an African night? Abigael got up and threw on a robe as she stepped onto her balcony.

The moon was still high enough to illuminate the impressive Ghost Mountain in the distance. A bird call split the night and overhead she saw the silent figure of an owl sailing through the air in search of prey. Strange noises and exotic smells assaulted her senses as she closed her eyes and lifted her head to the sky.

Taking a deep breath, she whispered, "Zeyde, help me. I am weak and need your help to stay the course and grab my future with both hands. I do like this man, Bryan. He says I look beautiful and those are words I never imagined a man saying to me. He makes me feel I can achieve anything, and he makes me feel special. Help me, Zeyde. Please."

A feeling of peace swept over her and for a moment she imagined her grandfather's presence was close by. "Oh Zeyde, you would love this country. There is so much poverty, but there is so much joy and beauty and love," she whispered to the spirit of her ancestors.

She peered over the balcony and saw luminous eyes looking back at her from the darkness. Laughing softly at her surprise and shock, she reminded herself she needed to get used to the idea of creatures of the night lurking in the underbrush. "No good getting scared of a small animal. Be brave, silly woman."

She awoke early the next morning to hear an eerie sound outside. Jumping up, she looked into the garden to see birds sticking their beaks onto the lawn.

"This is amazing." She rushed inside to find her robe and a glass of orange juice to sip while she observed this unusual spectacle.

Other birds joined the one and she looked in the sky to see a bright pink cloud. She made a note to ask Bryan what it might be. Then a kingfisher landed on the chair next to her and she caught her breath in wonder. As she moved, it flew off in fright. And then it was time to get ready. The sun was up, and she could hear movement from the hotel staff.

Arriving in the foyer, Bryan sat reading something on his laptop. "Ah, you are up. Good. We are going to stop at the supermarket in Mkuze if you need to stock up on things and then we will be on the road to Makatini and on to our latest project."

He smiled at her, and Abigael felt her heart do a flip of delight. "You might want to buy packets of candy. The kids in the village will love you forever if you give them sweeties. I heard somewhere when children's bones are still growing, they crave sweet things." Closing his laptop, he rose and gave her a quick peck on her cheek in greeting.

"Mm you smell good enough to eat." He whispered.

Abigael pursed her lips and said "It must be the mango I ate this morning."

"Nope, not mango. Something a bit spicier. Something uniquely you." He touched her cheek softly and all the hairs stood up on her arms as a shiver went down her spine. "I don't think it is a manufactured perfume, but rather something you give off naturally.' He laughed softly. "Sorry, I am useless at this romance and poetry stuff. But you do smell like happiness and joy. And I like it."

Rebecca and Carl arrived, and they all went into the dining room for breakfast to feed their bodies for the trip ahead. Rebecca smiled sweetly at her, and it took a moment for Abigael to remember the things she said the night before. Squaring her shoulders, Abigael put her hand on Bryan's arm and walked with him towards the buffet table.

Rebecca loaded her plate with crunchy bacon. "This is delicious, Abi; you should try some."

Grinning at her competitor, Abigael said, "Oh no, Becks, my grandfather would turn in his grave if I did."

As they sat down at the table, Rebecca leaned over. "Bryan, you said something interesting the other day about giving a hand up and not a handout. What did you mean? I want to learn all there is to know about living in Africa."

"Well, it's best to give you an example of what I mean. My parents saved for all us kids' education. When we completed our studies, we committed to paying a tenth of our income into the account to fund a scholarship for others who can't afford it. But what my dad and Mom do is to expect those students to work during the holidays to pay for their living costs. My folks pay the course fees and even give them a few sets of clothes each year, but it is an expectation they come back to work in their communities once they have graduated." He smiled at Rebecca and then said, "Many of these kids are from families where the parents are absent or not financially able to help. But you would be amazed at what they do. The family will arrive at my parents' door with offerings of baskets or bead work. A few will have a chicken or some crops to give. Most of the time my parents send them off with more than they arrived with. But at no time, do they feel they are beggars, and we are the saviours."

"What about a bank loan or government help?" Rebecca asked with a look of concern on her face.

"Well sadly, those are not always an option for these kids." Bryan shook his head at the thought.

Carl got up. "Enough talking folks, we need to be on the road before the heat of the day sets in."

They bid farewell to the Ghost Mountain Inn, with none of them having seen the eerie lights during the night and Abigael was not prepared to tell them she peered at the mountain in an expectation of seeing the visitation of ghosts until her eyes grew weary.

By the time they went to the small supermarket and swapped vehicles, the day heated, and Abigael was glad she was wearing a soft cotton top over her shorts. Anything more would be oppressive. Even with the battery-operated fan and a packet of extra batteries for future use, they sweated their way over the mountain and towards the small town of Josini close to the Pongolapoort dam.

"Have you ever heard about the author H Rider Haggard? No? Well, he lived here for a while and wrote his book, 'She', about the area. The title character was Ayesha, who was also called 'She who must be obeyed'. My Dad says she was a feminist of the Victorian era. A female of authority, if you will." He turned his head slightly as he smiled. "And today you will meet her real-life equivalent. Thandi Gumede is our tribal chief and yes, she is a female of authority."

"Oh, come on, mate." Carl chipped in. "Thandi is nothing like the awful woman in the book. And yes, I have read it. Don't give these women any false information, Bryan. Thandi is lovely and kind."

"Ah yes, but we disobey her at our peril." Bryan laughed. The closer they got to the project, the more at ease he seemed. He was obviously in his element and Abigael could see why he did not want to leave it. He knew every twist and turn of the road and seemed to expect the occasional cow to wander onto the dusty road. Small Zulu herders close at hand and waved as they drove past.

Bryan slowed right down and stopped at one point to show them a herd of elephants standing in the middle of some thorn trees. Abigael happily took photos and leaned forward in her backseat so she could get a better view. Rebecca looked a bit scared and asked if the elephants were dangerous. "Shouldn't we drive on in case they attack us?" she asked breathlessly.

"No, they are fine. There are no flapping ears and no signs of aggression at all. If there was, I would be the first one to drive off at speed. No one enjoys staring down the trunk of an angry animal as large as a small house." Bryan agreed.

He turned around. "How are you, Abigael? Not scared, are you?"

"Oh no. This is better than all those wildlife programs my grandpa and I would watch each week. Amazing." She said without taking her eyes off the pachyderms and their small children hidden between their legs.

They drove on, but the image of the family group of elephants stayed with Abigael for the rest of the day and haunted her dreams at night.

Finally, they arrived at Thandi's village, and she stood gleaming with happiness as the vehicle stopped in a cloud of dust.

"Bryan, Carl, it is so good to see you. And you have brought me some female company. How nice." Thandi stepped forward to greet them. She held out both hands as she offered them a smile and a welcome. "Welcome to my village. You will sleep in the contractor's enclosure, but in the meantime, let me take you to my hut for some cooling drinks and a bit of food."

Abigael and Rebecca followed obediently behind her as the men unloaded the supplies and their luggage from the vehicle.

Thunder clouds gathered above their heads and some of the youngsters helped Carl and Bryan unload the supplies.

There were a few people around and some youngsters clambered to touch the two women. Abigael remembered what Bryan told her about children and reached into her bag for some sweets. Thandi laughed when she saw the joy on the children's faces at Abigael's gift.

"You would think these children never saw a sweet in their lives. I got home two weeks ago with a huge packet of assorted candy, and do you know what? It's all gone? Gobbled up and devoured by the hungry hoards." Thandi admitted as she gently patted a child on his head.

A beautiful young girl hung onto Thandi's skirt and peeked out from behind the material as they stood waiting for the children to have their fill of sugary treats. Thandi pulled her forward. "This is my daughter, Paris. She is a bit shy of you because she doesn't see European women very often."

The little girl with one finger in her mouth and looked to be about four years of age. "I was studying at Oxford when I met her father. And Paris is where we went on honeymoon and where young Paris started her life journey." Thandi told them. "Her father lives in Kenya with his other wives and children. I wanted to come home to where I grew up and we have agreed to live this way. But you do not want to know about my marriage issues, do you? Come, let us get out of the heat and relax before the storm arrives." She led them into a large mud hut with golden thatching grass as a roof and a floor shining with a strange golden gleam. Sinking to the floor where a few pillows were scattered round, Thandi patted the pillows on both sides of her in invitation.

"My sister and mother have made some special drinks for you ladies after your long drive. They will be here in a moment. Is there anything I can help you with? Questions?" The two women joined her on the floor.

Thunder and lightning raged around them and for a moment, no one could speak for the pounding of the storm. Bryan and Carl rushed inside, shaking rain drops from their heads.

There seemed to be no furniture at all inside the hut and Abigael was tempted to ask her why there were no chairs. But she held her tongue and smiled instead. "Will we also sleep in a hut like this, Thandi?" she asked.

"I will let Bryan introduce you to your sleeping arrangements. But no, because most of our visitors are Europeans, they have set up hammocks. There were a few incidents where women ran screaming from their beds with nothing more than a dash of perfume to hide their modesty and a scream when they were visited by some creature or other in the middle of the night. And it's when Bryan invested in hammocks to remove the problem." Thandi laughed at the memory of the night. "I think Carl enjoyed seeing the naked women dashing around like chickens with no heads, but Bryan is a bit more traditional and said it was inappropriate to take advantage of their fears."

Bryan and Carl laughed with them as Thandi's family came in bearing calabashes full of drinks and platters full of delicious fruit, all cut into bite-sized pieces. Abigael's mouth watered as she waited to be offered the sustenance. The road was long and hot and with nothing more than a bottle of water and the long-digested breakfast to keep her going; she was hungry. The meal was perfect. There were a few fruits she'd never eaten, but others were familiar to the ones she tried the day before. She tasted them all. Some were fried in a sticky syrup and others made into a fresh fruit salad with lemon juice sprinkled over them. The small bowls given to them to use were carved from wood and as smooth as silk to the touch.

The storm was growing softer as it swept across the countryside and left their area steaming and heating up in the afternoon sunshine.

Thandi spoke to the men and asked if they'd gained the promised hydraulic pump? "Oh yes, she is a beauty, Thandi. And we got a good deal because we bought two of them. The company gave us some extra piping and clamps and even a few taps thrown in free. We were like children in Santa's workshop. I don't think Carl wanted to leave the place. He kept on asking if we could buy more stuff." Bryan laughed as his friend punched him on the arm.

"You were as bad as I was, Bryan. I saw you eyeing up those drills and the Archimedes screw mechanism. Aha, I saw you were enthralled and drooling slightly with lust over the workings." Carl answered.

"Oh yes, the Archimedes screw is perfect for another job we have planned for the end of the year. But what I really loved was the new technology connected to solar power and even a windmill geared towards smaller projects. Not much use here, Thandi. You need the maximum yield and not a piddly sized one. But it made me think of what is possible." Bryan admitted.

Abigael leaned forward as she listened to this discussion. Should she tell them she wrote the manual for the piddling, small windmill? It fascinated her when she was asked to write a simple how-to step-by-step instruction pamphlet. And yes, it was geared towards the small homesteader and not a large community project. She spent a few happy weeks talking to farmers about what information they would need to assemble it themselves without outside help. Not an easy task, but achievable with a bit of ingenuity.

Rebecca butted into the conversation to say, "My Dad has an Archimedes screw on our well. It works a dream unless you turn it upside down and then it's a disaster. My brother found out the hard way." She grinned as she said, "My Dad is keen to buy an Archimedes turbine to deal with our sewerage. And it needs to be installed upside down, he says. Just don't get them mixed up."

Abigael bit her lip as she wanted to jump in and tell them about the benefits of using it for electricity. For all she knew, they were well versed in all this information, and she would tell them things they already knew.

Bryan looked over at Abigael. Surprised, she'd commented little on the machinery. He knew read her work history and the knowledge she was keeping to herself. Perhaps she didn't want to sound like a know-it-all. Humility was a rare commodity, and he was glad to see Abigael was not mouthing off about her skill sets.

He stood up. "Time to show you where you will live for the next few days, ladies. Come along Carl, jump to it. Thank you Thandi for the delicious snack. Can we inspect the dam your people have been digging later this afternoon? I want to see if it will be deep enough for what I am envisioning."

"Sure Bryan. The workers will be so proud to show you what they have achieved. They are thrilled with the progress and are eager to see it benefit their families."

Bryan put out his hand to help Abigael up first and then Rebecca. He felt the soft skin of Abigael's hand and an urge to pull her closer washed over him, but he stopped himself in time. He knew he'd to give them both an equal chance at this. Whatever this turned out to be. He knew Carl preferred Rebecca, but for the life of him, he couldn't see what his business partner and friend saw in her. With her outstanding qualities on paper looking like they should work, and yet, there was something not quite right with her.

He led their small party to the construction workers' encampment. It was barely a five minutes' walk from the village. Their equipment was behind thick thorn bush walls and with a locked gate. There might be no criminals from the tribe, but it did not mean outsiders would not take advantage of the treasures inside. They'd a large truck and trailer housing a workshop and a diesel-powered generator. With a flick of a switch, the inside of the trailer could be transformed into a modern space to use a lathe or change a spare part. They even boasted a laser cutter for those jobs requiring it. Solar power was funneled down from the roof of the truck, where it was festooned with the best and most efficient of what was on offer. Between the Tezla wall and the generator, they were self-sufficient and ready for whatever engineering issues were thrown at them. Plans were carefully stacked in cubby holes and a satellite dish allowing communication with the world. Bryan felt quite proud of the organised area and opened the large rear doors with a feeling of excitement to see what Abigael would think.

He was not disappointed. She did not say a word as she walked from work bench to desk and back again, touching the lathe and the tools and nodding her head. "It is fantastic, Bryan. Your engineers must be thrilled to work in such an organised workshop. I know I would be in seventh heaven if I worked here." The smile on her face lit up with an internal joy beautiful to see. "You have tools here I haven't seen in a long time. Just look at this. This dogleg reamer. Wow. Stork beak pliers. I am so excited, it's almost like Hanukkah has come early and filled my stocking with fun toys to play with." She picked up a tool and held it to her cheek. "A Cape Chisel. Just what you need to get mud out of grooves."

Her enthusiasm was infectious, and Carl and Bryan ferreted out their own personal favorites.

Bryan held up a tool he would never be without. "This is essential for this job, a Stubby

Nail Eater. It has helped me drill through some really tough pieces of wood full of old nails."

Carl was not to be outdone and held up his preference. "I personally favour the Spud Wrench. Wrench on one end and drift pin on the other."

Bryan looked around to see where Rebecca was and saw her sitting at the desk, fiddling with the laptop computer. "What do you enjoy, Rebecca?" He asked.

"Well, my brothers always told me I should have a sky hook in case my tools fell down the well. But I think they were joking with me." She smiled at them all and went back to the computer.

"Funnily enough, there is such a tool. Aircraft mechanics use it to stop their tools from falling into the engine compartment. I think we have one somewhere over here?" Bryan looked at the tool board above the bench. "Yup, this is it right here." He held it out to Rebecca, but she seemed to have lost interest in the discussion as she opened the internet.

They spent a few happy moments discovering new treasures Abigael was excited to see. Rebecca cleared her throat. "Not to be rude, but I need to use the lady's facilities. Where do I find them?"

"Oops sorry. I get carried away. It's just as well you are here to remind us of our manners. Come this way." Bryan led them down the steel steps and around the back behind the truck to where there was a bank of portable toilets and showers. "All the mod cons at your convenience, madam." He pointed the way and then left the women to find their own way to the facilities.

Rebecca looked horrified but didn't say a word. Bryan smiled to himself. If the idea of going to the toilet in such simple surroundings was not to her liking, then maybe Carl was wrong about who would adapt and who would not.

Carl waited for him at the truck. "You know, Abigael is pretty special. She knows her stuff. But give her a few days without indoor plumbing and we will separate the girls from the real women." He smiled at his friend. "It's a pity we don't have those beds on the floor anymore. It might be fun to see the two women go head-to-head in a naked race under the stars."

Bryan smiled at the image this statement conjured up. "I think Abigael is the type of woman who wears shorts and a t-shirt to sleep in. I am not sure if either of them sleeps in the buff like those Norwegian volunteers did. Those male volunteers got a genuine thrill the night the women rampaged through the camp in nothing but perfume and screams. And as did you, if I remember correctly."

When the women rejoined them, Bryan led the way to their dormitory sleeping area. The simple building was made from mud brick and thatch, but inside there were various hammocks slung between poles and beautiful woven mats next to each bed. There were at least ten hammocks but at the moment they were between volunteer tourists. They'd to be orientated by a government agency before starting their work for the company and it was still in progress. In four or five weeks, the room would be a hive of activity, with languages from all corners of the world. A similar structure housed the male volunteers and was similarly empty of occupants.

"Choose whichever hammock takes your fancy. We have an outdoor shower set up under the trees behind a cloth enclosure for you to use. Although, as you noticed, we have the portable ones set up. When we have a full complement of volunteers, every facility is used and necessary. Do you want to come down to the dam with us? It is near to here and usually we walk, but today we will take the four-wheel drive. We have some tools needing to be delivered and it is not worth taking them down piecemeal."

Abigael put her suitcases down next to a hammock close to the door and Rebecca chose one in a sheltered corner. As they both turned towards the men, Bryan was interested to note the difference in attitude between them. Abigael almost bounced in her excitement, while Rebecca strolled down the room at a leisurely pace.

"It's no use getting all hot and sweating by rushing around like crazy people, Abi." Rebecca admonished her fellow female.

Thandi waited for them next to the vehicle and with Paris clasped to her hip. "Do you mind if this little one comes along, Bryan? It will be a squeeze, but there should be room for all of us."

"I tell you what, Thandi. How about we let Paris drive?" He winked outrageously at Thandi and the little child. "You can sit on my lap and guide us with the steering wheel, and I will make sure we go slow enough to stop if we need to." Bryan suggested.

"Oh yes, Bryan. Can I? Please Mom?" Paris and her shyness were separated as she embraced the idea of driving the vehicle.

"As long as Bryan promises he will not speed. And I will sit right next to you to make sure he listens to me." She insisted.

Carl said, "Well, I will walk and leave you lazy bones to drive in luxury." He laughed as he started running. "I bet you I can beat the lot of you to the dam." he called over his shoulder.

It took a few minutes before Thandi was happy with the driving arrangements and then they proceeded down a bush track and into a shallow area and along an open patch. They could see Carl running like the wind in front of them and Bryan said to Paris, "Shall we try to catch him? Do you think if I go faster, you can steer the truck?"

She nodded her head happily and Bryan carefully kept his hands on the wheel below where she gripped. Paris stood in the floor space between Bryan's knees and could barely see through the windscreen. "Faster Bryan, faster. He is getting away." Paris screeched.

All the adults laughed along with the little girl's excitement. "He will get tired Paris, and then we will pass him easily." Bryan promised.

As they drew level with Carl, Bryan eased off on the accelerator and opened his window. "Do you want a ride, mate?" He teased.

"This heat saps my energy. I tell you what, I will let Thandi sit on my lap and then we will all get there safely." Carl flirted.

"Oh no, Carl. I have no interest in sitting on your lap. You can sit in the back with all the tools." Thandi insisted with a grin. "It's not far now. Or else you can squeeze in between the two women. They are so skinny you can fit in easily." She suggested.

"Ah, now, it sounds appealing. A thorn between two beautiful roses." Carl jumped up on the step of the truck and opened the door next to Abigael, climbing over her as the vehicle continued on at its leisurely pace down the track.

It usually took half an hour to walk to the work site, and at the rate they drove, it took almost as long in the vehicle. They were greeted by a group of happy youngsters gathered around a large area excavated by hand and hard work. In the center of the dam area, two young men wrestled in the mud created by the recent storm. Yells and cat calls were encouraging this display of strength. Thandi stepped from the landrover. "What are you all doing? Alpheus, Simon, stop wrestling and come talk to me this instance."

The two young men stopped dead in their tracks and turned towards their leader with heads hung low. A beautiful Zulu girl stepped forward. "Auntie Thandi, it is not their fault. They both want to prove they are the strongest. Some of us girls are the judges and the one who wins gets a kiss from each of us at the end."

"Is this true? Alpheus? Explain yourself." Thandi stood with her hands on her hips and Abigael could see why the men said she was not someone you would disobey. Within a few minutes, the problem was sorted out and Alpheus and Simon were instructed their punishment was to unload the tools in the back of the vehicle.

Bryan and Carl busily inspected the bottom of the excavation. "Abigael, could you find the theodolite?" Bryan called.

A quick inspection of the back of the vehicle and Abigael joined the men with the electronic tool. She smiled. "What do you want to measure? I can do it if you want to continue discussing the issues."

Five minutes later, the measurements were done and logged onto the digital device. As Abigael stood looking down at the numbers, Bryan walked up next to her and put his hand on her shoulder as he peered at the measurements. "A little deeper in this corner and a lot deeper in the middle should do it, Bryan,'" Abigael suggested.

Rebecca leaned against the Land rover and watched them from her perch. Her eyes narrowed as she watched the interaction. She waved at them, but Abigael got the distinct impression she was not happy to see how Bryan relied on Abigael to do the measurements on her own.

Bryan slid his hand down Abigael's spine and settled in the small of her back as he continued to observe the digital numbers. The feeling of his warm hand sent shivers through Abigael's body, and she physically stopped herself from leaning into him. She felt the brush of his breath on the top of her head, and it felt good to be so close to him. He moved his hand to her arm, and it was like a caress as he positioned his body, so his torso melded into hers. Her arm and side flamed with feeling as she glanced up at him. He looked right into her eyes, and she felt the breath catch in her throat. It was the most intimate moment she ever experienced with someone of the opposite sex, and it thrilled her to her core. Bryan smiled. "Thank you for helping."

It took a few seconds for her to find the strength to reply. "Sure Bryan. I love working in the field and this is right up my alley."

She could not say how they got back to camp. All Abigael could think of was Bryan and the excitement surging through her like wildfire. Rebecca and she were in their sleeping area when suddenly Rebecca said, "I saw your blatant attempt at getting into Bryan's good books, Abi. Just because you know one end of a theodolite from another doesn't mean you will win."

Abigael shook herself to focus on what her roommate said. "Rebecca, I was not trying to get into his good books. I enjoy this sort of work."

But Rebecca was eager to get her viewpoint heard and continued on. "And those showers. Well, when we get married, I will tell him in no uncertain terms I expect more respect. A home with proper walls and floors and definitely a decent bathroom. Not even you, miss goody two shoes, will be happy with this situation for long. Mark my words." She flung herself onto her hammock and rolled over to turn her back towards Abigael.

But later, Rebecca was sweetness and laughter as Bryan and Carl roasted meat and vegetables over an open fire. She enthused about the purity of the bush life and Abigael wondered if what she'd heard earlier was even the truth. Rebecca sat as close to Bryan as she could get. Jumping up to get him a cold drink when she saw his was low and even tucking a napkin into his collar to stop him from dripping meat juice onto his shirt. She laughed at his stories and asked questions. It seemed like Abigael might as well not even be there as the evening continued on.

"Bry, can you please take me for a walk in the wild? I have always dreamed of a walk on the wild side with a handsome man. And to be truthful, I am a little bit scared of the animals. But with you, I will be safe." Rebecca oozed a sexual invitation as she rubbed her body against his.

Totally confused at the way the night developed, Bryan went along with her request and shrugged an apologetic farewell as the two of them wandered off into the night. Carl sat back and looked at Abigael. "Interesting. She is a bit of a minx. You will have your work cut out for you to get her claws out of your man, Abigael."

"Oh Carl, he is not my man. He is the one who has to decide who he wants to marry, and I don't think I have a snowball's chance in hell at winning this race." Abigael admitted.

"Abigael. What are you talking about? I know my friend, and, in all conscience, I have to tell you. You have always been his first choice. I insisted we bring Rebecca along, so he at least would be sure of what he wants. Or should I say, of who he wants?" He smiled at Abigael. "I was worried a city girl would not be good for my mate. But I was wrong. You are a perfect couple. And who am I to stand in the way of a match made in Heaven?"

But later, when Rebecca returned, she stood next to Abigael's hammock. "He kissed me; you know. A proper kiss. I didn't expect any fireworks, but he is pretty gorgeous, and I loved being in his arms." She smirked as she continued. "He put his arm around me and held me tight."

In the men's sleeping area, Bryan told a totally different story. "Carl, she kept saying she was scared and could I put my arm around her. An owl hooted and she literally jumped into my arms and then started kissing me. What on earth am I supposed to do?" Bryan asked.

"Honestly, you can enjoy the journey and see how far she wants to take this. Or tell her you are not interested and send her packing. I know what I would do, but it is up to you, mate. Be a man and stand up for yourself for once. You will find happiness with a girl with your best interests at heart and Rebecca is a man-eater, if ever I have seen one." Carl admitted as he pulled the sheet over his head. "Now go to bed and leave me to my dreams of leggy blondes."

Bryan stood next to his friend for a moment and then went back outside and into the mobile workshop. He always thought clearly with a tool in his hands. He dared not use the lathe or any of the electric tools, but he grabbed a small carving knife and started whittling a piece of wood. He made a doll for Paris and started the project a few months earlier. All he needed to complete was the features on the face. A delicate hand was required for this task, and with the added benefit of allowing his mind to wander as he worked. He learned his skills from an accomplished Zulu carver near his home. As a boy, he enjoyed the days spent at the feet of the master as they conversed in Zulu about all the woes of the world. How he wished he could go back and ask his old friend for his advice now.

But as he carved the lips, a clarity came to his mind. It was almost as if he could see into the future. A future peopled by his own children sitting at his feet. Children who at the moment bore no features but who he knew in his heart belonged to him and Abigael. Pushing his shoulders back, he knew he was decided. Tomorrow morning, he would tell Rebecca she needed to return to America.

At breakfast, Rebecca was upbeat and laughing at everything. She even smiled at the idea of showering under the spreading Marula tree with its accompaniment of monkeys peering at her from the branches. When Bryan asked if he could have a word with her, she turned and smiled at Abigael in what he could only imagine was a look of victory.

"Rebecca, I have decided about who I want to spend my life with. And I am sorry, but it is not you. I know this might come as a shock, but I have decided. I know I promised you three weeks in Africa, and I aim to live up to the commitment I made. I will ask Carl to drive you back to Sun City and you may join a tour group or fly down to Cape Town to see the sights. I am happy to pay your costs of your return flight and can only offer you my apologies if I have misled you." Bryan finished his prepared speech in a rush.

"Oh Bryan, what have I done to make you treat me this way? You cannot really choose Abi over me? Really? She is fat and ugly, and she will not be good for you. I will help you to be a success. We could have a lovely home somewhere and you could commute to this wild camp whenever you desired. I would never hold you back." Rebecca pleaded. "We could train someone to do this grunt work for you. Maybe start a chain of camps throughout the country? You could be the managing director and never lift a finger." She batted her eyelashes as if her words were all he was hoping to hear.

But Bryan felt his heart clench at the thought of what she wanted. "No, Rebecca, it's not what I envision my future to be. I actually like doing the grunt work and being in touch with the projects. And to be a success? Well, I do pretty well out of what I do. I have a roof over my head and money in the bank. In this part of the world, it makes me one of the rich and privileged."

"Yes Bry, I know you think you are a success. But with my help, we could be so much more." Rebecca grabbed his hand and placed it on her breast. "Feel this Bry. You could have this instead of the milk cow of a woman you have chosen."

"Rebecca, enough. This is over. Go pack your bags and I will tell Thandi you are leaving. Hopefully, you will be at Ghost Mountain in time for you to enjoy a spa and a massage this afternoon'" Bryan insisted.

Tears sprang in her eyes as she pouted. "Please think this through Bry. I am all your dreams wrapped in one. I cannot go home a loser. My family will never let me forget it if I don't get married to my African millionaire."

"Millionaire? Who told you I was a millionaire?" Bryan asked, surprised.

"I spent some time on the Internet and there was a newspaper article about a year ago listing you as one of the top millionaire bachelors' of South Africa. Did you think I would come to this continent without first making sure of what I was getting into?" she smiled in confidence. "You were only number nine on the list, but together we can change it. Please, think about what you are giving up and for whom."

But her pleas fell on deaf ears as Bryan wondered if it was why the two women agreed to join him in Africa? Suddenly, he questioned his foolproof plan of finding someone who would love him for himself. "Does Abigael feel the same way, Rebecca?"

"Well, obviously. I researched her too and she comes from a wealthy family in New York. Why would she agree to this silly contract of marriage and work if she didn't expect to get something out of it?" Rebecca stood with her hands on her hips as she observed the reaction her statement had on Bryan. "She is a clever little puss."

Sighing deeply, Bryan gathered his thoughts. "Well, regardless, you need to pack and leave with Carl in an hour."

Carl and Bryan discussed this option early this morning on their daily walk to the dam and both agreed it was for the best.

Rebecca pursed her lips together. "Well, if it's what you want, then I suppose I'd better go and pack. I don't suppose you could introduce me to any rich unmarried men. If I can find a husband, then I will not be the laughingstock of my family."

Bryan felt like rolling his eyes at her but stopped himself just in time.

"I am sorry Rebecca; find your own rich husband. But I can pay for a luxury holiday and hopefully you can meet someone nice you can love."

Now it was Rebecca's turn to roll her eyes at him. "I have tried it all before Bry. Those men on luxury holidays want a quick roll in the hay and not much more. Oh well, a holiday would be nice."

She turned on her heel and stormed off towards the sleeping quarters without so much as a backward glance.

Later, as he stood alongside Abigael watching Rebecca and Carl drive off into the distance, he took her hand in his and wove his fingers through hers. "What would you like to do today, Abigael?" He felt the thrill of being with her rush through his body and a desire to find out all he could about her.

She turned to him. "I want to see the area and all it offers. Plants, animals, minerals and people. I saw some interesting rocks yesterday; they looked like crystals. Gosh Bryan, I don't really care what we do as long as it is with you."

Carl took their primary means of transport to drive back to town and they were now reliant on using a beat-up old utility vehicle. Bryan led Abigael to this truck and handed her in. "Crystals. Well, I know just the place." He climbed behind the wheel. They bumped over and through the sandy tracks making up the roads in the area and were far from the camp in an area dotted with strange, yellow-coloured trees. "Fever trees. Back in the early 1900's the farmers thought the trees were the harbingers of fever. They did not know it was the mosquito causing the malaria. This is the only tree in the world to produce chlorophyll with photosynthesis through its bark and not only via the leaves. Rudyard Kipling wrote about it. I grew up with the stories he told called Just-So Stories." He stopped the truck and turned towards Abigael, taking her hands in his. "There was an elephant child who wanted to know what crocodiles ate. He went down to the grey-green, greasy Limpopo River all set about with fever trees." He smiled at the memory. "Rudyard Kipling started telling stories to his daughter every night and she insisted he never vary from the words she found so fascinating. Apparently, she loved the alliteration of greasy and grey-green and would giggle as her father repeated them for her. He later made them into a book and illustrated them himself."

"There were stories about the kangaroo and how he got his tail. The camel and how he got his hump because he was lazy. But definitely for me, it was always the story of the Elephant and how he got his trunk." Bryan turned towards the interesting-colored trees. "They are amazing trees, aren't they?"

Abigael stared at him, fascinated as he repeated the story of his childhood. "They like to grow in groves and close to water. They sacrifice branches to absorb toxins and the weaver birds love to nest in its branches. In Christian legends, the thorny crown around Christ's head at the time of his crucifixion was from this tree." He took a breath as he gathered his thoughts. "Egyptians used its bark as a paint dye or sometimes the gum as a fragrance. Apparently, it represents the idea of rebirth. Perhaps because Christ is supposed to have risen from the dead."

He got out of the vehicle and stood next to the tree and held out his hand for Abigael to join him. "The Zulu uses it for medicinal purposes. It is potent as an antioxidant and good for gut health. There are some anti-microbial properties in the bark. A tea made from the bark helps with sleep problems and scientists have found it works with brain chemistry. Good for brain disorders." He looked at Abigael and smiled. "Not something you need to worry about."

Bryan pulled her closer and Abigael came into his arms. She wound her arms behind his neck as he looked down at her with wonder. "I think I am falling in love with you, Abigael. I know I want to be with you. Now and forever if possible." He bent his head closer to hers and allowed his lips to play across hers. "Please say something, Abigael. I am dying here wondering if you feel the same way."

She let her head fall back as she smiled up into his eyes. "Bryan." she whispered. "You make me tingle all over and I feel good when I am with you. I smile when I think of you and every time, I glimpse you. Is it falling in love? If it is, then yes, I think I feel the same way as you do."

He took a deep breath and lowered his head, so they stood nose to nose. "Abigael Rabinowitz, please marry me and make me the happiest man alive?"

"Oh, I don't know Bryan Bond. You didn't get down on bended knee and I am told by those in authority it is the required method of proposals." Abigael laughed as Bryan immediately dropped to his knee.

She sank to the ground with him. "Silly man, I am not a traditional girl and being on bended knee is not a requirement in my books." Abigael tilted forward and before they knew what happened, they were fallen over, and she laid on top of him under the spread of Fever trees on the banks of a small river in the middle of the African bush.

He allowed his hands to wander over her back as he stared up at her. "When do you want to get married? And do you want to fly your family out here, or should we fly back to the States? There is only one problem. I don't think I can wait too long to become your husband. Please. Like tomorrow would be good." He begged.

Abigael sat back on her haunches and felt his response to her closeness. She blushed bright red as she shook her head. "Tomorrow, maybe not but the day afterwards is a possibility. Don't we have to get a license or something?"

Bryan grunted, "Yes, licenses and stuff. Oh, my word, this is going to be agony if I have to wait much longer." He flipped Abigael over, so he towered above her. "This definitely qualifies as lust in the dust, my sweet lady. Lots of lust and plenty of dust."

Pulling her upright, they returned to the truck and back on their way to the crystals he promised to show her before they become distracted by the Fever trees and each other. This time, Abigael snuggled up close to Bryan and it took all his concentration to remember what they were supposed to be doing. They found the rock formation he searched for and laughed as they clambered over the outcrop to find the perfect sample for her to take back with her. Sunlight flashed through the crystal and the refracted light played rainbows across her face as the truck made its way back to camp.

Both Bryan and Abigael sent messages to their families about the upcoming nuptials. Stephen and Emma suggested a wedding at their farm. A distant uncle was a marriage celebrant and was happy to perform the ceremony. Zlota answered and said she and Rachel would be there.

Or "We will be there with bells on. Don't worry about a dress. I have the perfect one all picked out for you."

Bryan asked the uncle to organise the legal side of things and the date was set for five days ahead. Zlota and Rachel booked their tickets, and it would take at least as long for Bryan and Abigael to drive down to the family farm and get things sorted out. Carl was contacted and he was not in the least surprised. Rebecca settled into the Ghost Mountain Inn and already flirted with a local farmer. She'd said she wanted to go to Durban, and it fitted in with the plans Bryan and Carl already set in motion. A tour along the coast road to Cape Town was decided on and booked.

Carl said, "Look, I know I have the only decent vehicle here with me. But how about you drive the rust bucket to Mkuze and collect your car from there? I will drive the Land rover down to your parent's farm and meet you all."

"It sounds like a plan, Carl. Will you drive Rebecca to Durban before you go to my folks?" Bryan asked.

"Sure. And I can pick up a spare part we have been waiting for while I am in the city." The two business partners and friends decided on times and places and finished with farewells.

Bryan found Abigael sitting under the pergola sheltering the eating area and he leaned down to give her a kiss on the top of her head as he sat next to her and told her what was organised. Thandi and Paris came wandering over from their village holding a large bottle of a mixture of guava and pineapple juice.

"I saw Carl and the other woman leaving this morning and then the two of you vanished for the day. Is there anything you want to tell me, Bryan?" Thandi winked and gave a smile.

They told her their news and toasted their union with the fruit juice. Paris came and sat at Abigael's feet silently. Abigael touched the child's head with a gentle hand and the little girl lifted her face and smiled at Abigael. "It's nice when you touch my head, Miss Abi. You have a kind face." She announced, much to the amazement of her mother and Bryan.

"Well, high praise indeed, Abigael." Thandi said, "My daughter is not usually very accepting of strangers. In fact, she often runs and hides when anyone comes to visit."

Abigael took a few sweeties out of her pocket and offered them to Paris. And the little child chattered away about many things she found of interest.

The story of the Fever trees found its way into the conversations and Paris was fascinated as Abigael repeated large tracts of the stories. "When I am in the city, I will get you a set of Just So books Paris. They are all about animals and how they got their features."

"Oh Miss Abi, yes, it would be so nice. And then you can read them to me when you get back."

Abigael showed her the crystal they had collected, and she surprised them all with her comments about flaws and clarity.

"My Mom tells me they are not worth anything at all. But those Chinese people who wanted to buy some of the tribal land seemed very interested after Simon showed them the crystals."

"Really Paris? You didn't tell me. Anyhow, those Chinese businessmen left without my agreement to sell them our land." Thandi looked over at Bryan. "Do you think we should hire a geologist to check things out?"

Bryan thought about the crystals for a moment. "We have found a few geodes while working in this area. Amethyst usually, but this crystal looks more like Citrine. I think you would be wise to get a geologist. I could help you set up a tumbler to clean up some rocks to see if they have any fire inside them. Your tribe could make a few dollars selling them to dealers throughout the country. Heck, I am sure we could open an online shop for you, and we would train up your youngsters about the internet marketing stuff."

Both Thandi and Bryan looked enthused about this new idea and for the next hour, they spoke about what this would mean for the tribe.

As Thandi and a very sleepy Paris walked back to their home, Bryan turned to Abigael and smiled as he apologised. "Sorry. I get so enthusiastic sometimes, I forget everything else. Were you bored?" He got up from his camp chair and sank down in front of her and took her hands

in his. "I have not been a very good fiancé to
neglect you as I have."

Abigael shook her head at him. "It was
interesting to see you with your business hat on.
You really love this life and it's a good thing." She
touched his cheek and wiped a smudge of dust off
it with her thumb. "Never apologise for being
happy with your work. It is a privilege few people
have."

Bryan stood up and pulled her into his
arms. "Time for bed Miss Rabinowitz. The night
is well spent."

He felt her response to him in the way
she moved against him. She slid her hands into the
pockets at the back of his jeans and gently
squeezed his buttocks as she pressed her body to
his. "I have been wanting to feel your butt since
the moment I saw you." Abigael admitted. "I have
a thing about derrieres in blue jeans. And yours is
spectacular."

Bryan laughed delightedly. "Now don't
apologise for finding joy in my body. I plan to
introduce you too much, oh so much more
enjoyment." He put his hands in the back pockets
of her shorts and ran his hands over the contours
of her shape. "Mmm and your derriere is not too
shabby either, Abigael."

He bent his head over hers and kissed her
eyelids and then her nose tip. "I love your eyes
sparkling with happiness at the simple things in
life. And I love your nose wrinkling when you
smile." And then he kissed her lips and in between

pecks, he said, "And your mouth is so full and generous I want to devour it and discover all you can offer."

Abigael groaned in delight as the stars above her seemed to spin in the sky. Bryan undid the top button of her blouse and started kissing her collarbone. "And I love the freckles decorating your shoulders and peeping out of your blouse all day long." He undid another button and cupped her breast. "Your skin is soft as silk and as exotic as an Asian magic carpet. Oh goodness me woman, tell me to stop before I have you standing naked in front of me." He begged.

Bryan battled to control his desires as he looked down at the deep brown eyes staring back at him. They were like pools he could dive into and never resurface. "Do you want to wait for the wedding, Abigael? I can do this. I can be a good fiancé and not push you to do things you don't want to do right now." His blood beat through his head and he barely heard her reply.

"Bryan, I am a virgin. And yes, I am scared, but I know you will take care of me. I trust you." Abigael whispered as she reached up and undid his buttons.

Picking her up in his arms, he walked with her towards his room. He thanked all the Gods for a proper bed and knowing he would not need to deflower this woman in a rocking and swaying hammock. But he knew there would have been no stopping the tide of his passion even if he faced a hammock. Kicking open the door to his abode, he didn't bother switching on a light as he instinctively made his way to his bed. Not exactly the most romantic situation, a tiny room far from everything, but it was the best he could do in the situation.

Chapter Eight

bigael knew this night would change her life. And yet, she felt anxiety with the fear she might not be all Bryan could desire. She watched in the gloom as he divested himself of his shirt and then kicked off his shoes and undid his belt. For a moment, she wanted to close her eyes and then remembered what her grandfather said to enjoy every moment and experiences life threw at her. She saw the fine hair on his chest and felt an urge to run her fingers over his muscles. Bryan leaned over her and ran his fingers down between her breasts and undid the last of her buttons with one swift movement. Her blouse joined his clothing on the floor, and she caught her breath at the thought of what was to come. But she need not have worried because Bryan took his time. Kissing her body as he exposed it to the warm night air. Finally, he took off her shoes and it was all she could do to tell him to hurry and get it over with. He lay down on the bed next to her and started murmuring. Telling her how beautiful her body was.

"You are so soft; I fear hurting you, sweetheart." He teased her nipples, and she felt the electric thrill of his actions rush through her body and down between her legs. She arched her back and cried a visceral cry of passion.

"Bryan, stop teasing me. I am ready for you. Please." She begged.

As he slid his hand over her belly and to the core of her desire, she gasped in pleasure. And still Bryan continued his attack on her senses. He kissed her breasts and then moved his lips over her belly until she squirmed under his touch.

"Lie still Abigael. Let me enjoy you for a while longer. We have all night. There is no one to interrupt us." And lie still, she did as her breath rasped in her throat.

A wave of ecstasy rose through her body as he brought her closer and closer to the edge of reason. At last, he rose above her and slipped inside her body. He lay still for a moment as he allowed her body to adjust to this new and exciting experience.

They moved in unison, riding the crest of the waves of desire until Abigael felt her mind leave her body in a flight of delight and sensory overload. She grasped his hips and held him to her for a moment as she enjoyed the surges of energy. He allowed her to have her moment of joy before moving slowly and sinuously above her until he to found his release. It was more than he ever expected and certainly he'd never felt this thrill with any other woman. But he didn't share this insight with Abigael. He thought she might not want to know about the women in his past.

After the first mind blowing sexual journey, Abigael lay catching her breath as he pulled her close to him and cradled her to his heaving chest. "Did I hurt you, sweetheart?"

Abigael laughed in relief. There was no pain or discomfit. "No, you didn't hurt me, Bryan. But you changed my life. You were marvelous. When can we do it again?"

Now it was Bryan's turn to laugh. "You are a naughty girl, Abigael. I thought you would be freaked out and here you are asking for more."

Suddenly, Abigael sat up. "Oops, sorry, I seem to have left a wet puddle on your sheets."

"No, no need to worry. It's the physical reaction to the lovemaking and it shows we both enjoyed ourselves. Relax. We will hopefully add to the puddle before morning." Bryan pulled her back into his arms as he smiled at her discomfit. "You are an unusual woman. Abigael and I love you for being who you are."

The night flew by and as Abigael watched the sunrise through the window, she rolled over on top of Bryan and kissed his flushed face. "I think I need a cold shower before we go out into the world. Otherwise, everyone will see on my face we have been making love all night."

Bryan grabbed her and whispered, "Don't be gone long, Abigael. I miss you already."

She didn't bother with clothes and walked out of his room naked as on the day she was born. She strolled across the yard towards her own hammock, totally oblivious of a care or concern of being discovered without clothes. She hummed a cheerful tune as she collected her t-shirt and jeans for the day and then strode to the outside shower. She opened the tap, when the door was pulled open, and an equally naked Bryan stepped in.

"Do you mind if we save water and shower together?" he asked with a cheeky grin.

"I think this is what you referred to as lust in the dust Bryan, except it will be mud in a moment if we don't watch out." Abigael commented as Bryan lathered her up with definite sexual intent.

"We can always shower again. The reservoir is quite large, and we don't have to be on the road for a while."

They finally finished their prolonged shower and got on the road as the sun rose in the sky. The old truck was so noisy there was no chance of talking, and Abigael happily sang quietly to herself as they drove. Two hours later, they reached the small town and could park the rusty relic and climb into the much more commodious Mercedes Benz. Neither one of them thought of a meal and they were hungry. Bryan knew of a small restaurant to sell them a take-away meal. Which is what they did. They stopped in a layby overlooking a large river and Bryan laid their meal on the hood of the car.

Vehicles rushed past on the highway and a few people tooted in greeting as they enjoyed their delicious late breakfast. It was as they were packing up when Abigael thought to ask about his family. She was focusing on Bryan so much over the past week she did not know what situation she might walk into. "Are your family going to accept me, Bryan? I am not exactly what your parents would choose for a wife."

"Oh, heck yeah, they have already heard everything about you. I even sent them a photo I took yesterday at the Fever tree grove. Don't you worry about a thing. If I am happy, my parents will accept of you."

Shaking off the crumbs of their repast, they returned to the highway and drove past vast plantations of pine trees. And then the pine trees turned to sugar cane farms and still they drove. Every now and again Bryan would tell the stories of the towns they passed. He seemed well versed in all the history of the area and the tribal politics of the time. Abigael enjoyed watching him as he became animated about poverty amongst such abundance. They drove past a university nestled in the Zululand hills and the importance of encouraging future generations to become self-sufficient and not rely on handouts. This was obviously something close to his heart as he gesticulated at the stupidity of politicians.

And then they turned along a lesser highway and again the land changed. There were still sugarcane fields, but now the countryside was peppered by African homes with subsistence farmers and their small blocks of cultivated fields. Bryan became pensive as they passed the signpost for Ulundi, the royal residence of the Zulu ruling family. They took the longer route along the coastal road and Bryan obviously wanted her to see the different scenery. Again, the countryside changed, and now the ancient trees of Nkandla shaded the road as they slowed down for the sharp corners and gentle dips and curves in the journey.

"Abigael, this to me is the heart and soul of Zululand. Supernatural being lived within the Nkandla Forest. No, don't look surprised. After all, I am part Zulu, and my Zulu part becomes stronger the closer we get to my home." Bryan smiled again at her look of confusion. "Didn't you research who I was before you flew out to South Africa? I know Rebecca certainly did, and she assured me you did too."

"Good grief Bryan. Why? Unless there is some deep, dark secret you have been hiding from me? Six wives and twenty children, perhaps?"

"No. No wives or children. My father is part Zulu, and I am used to the racial slurs on my journeys. I don't want you to be surprised by my history, Abigael. And know you can always ask me whatever you want about my past." He assured her, happy to know she wasn't judging him for his money or even his family history.

"I suppose we all have skeletons in our closets. When you meet my grandmother one day, she will tell you all about the holocaust and the terrible things the Nazi's did to our family. And I am quite used to being judged by others because of the accident of my birth. Rebecca told me you would not want to marry me because of my faith. But I ignored her words and go with my gut. Well, more than my gut because by then I was already under your spell and imagining many sexual things." Abigael laughed. "Yes Bryan, women have fantasies about those sorts of things. No need to look so shocked."

She leaned across the divide between their seats and gave him a quick kiss on his cheek as he returned to his driving.

The forest was indeed beautiful and spiritual. It reminded her of a photo she saw once of a cathedral in Spain. All curves and unusual shapes but mixed with a reverence for God. Birds flitted between the green canopy, and she was sure she glimpsed wild deer grazing amongst the trees. Bryan slowed right down so she could observe this marvel of the ancient world alongside a modern highway.

"It's great, isn't it?" Bryan opened his window and the perfume of leaves and living plants wafted through into the car. He took a deep breath. "Better than any man-made scent. Not an iota of artifice or chemical to be found." He grasped her hand in his and the two of them remained silent as they absorbed the surrounding atmosphere.

The forest gave way to a town, the anthesis of the beauty left behind. New houses and fancy cars, high walls and over-indulgence abounded. Bryan raised his eyebrows at Abigael. "And this results from new money spent unwisely."

He sped up slightly as they left this mixture of the old ways and the new and driving on country roads which were mainly dust and patches of tarmac. They returned down the highway towards the coast to reach Bond's drift and Bryan said, "I know I shouldn't be taking detours on our way to my home, but I really couldn't resist showing you the forest."

The sugarcane fields were once again stretched from horizon to horizon. They reached the town of Bond's Drift and again Bryan put on his tourist guide hat. "This is where my family first settled when they arrived from Norfolk in England. My great grandfather was the original Stephen Bond and helped the Great White Hunters of the day traverse the Tugela River. This was the last outpost of civilisation before they entered the wilds of Africa."

A lazy brown river flowed below them as they travelled along its banks. And then they turned down a farm road leading them away from history and into the future.

Driving through the gates of Bond's drift, she saw some strange cattle grazing alongside the road. They were like nothing she'd seen on her farm trips in America and were reminiscent of the longhorn cattle of Texas. She was once been asked to travel to the State for business and was in awe of their impressive horns. But these were almost as stately, and Bryan pulled the car over on the side of the road.

"This is my dad's pride and joy. He breeds the Nguni cattle, and these are descended from the ancient aurochs from over eight thousand years ago. They travelled down with the Nguni tribe, of which the Zulus are part, through the ages and have changed little over time. They were mixed with the Indian Zebu cattle to give a bit of diversity and strength. The Khoisan people, who were here before the Nguni tribes arrived, owned a breed of this bovine and they called them the Sanga cattle species. No doubt my father will bend your ear over the next few days and tell you about how the Egyptians have these same cattle painted on the tombs of their pharaohs." He looked at Abigael to see if she understood this monologue he knew almost by heart, having heard it a thousand times over the years.

"Really? These are your dad's cattle. They are beautiful." Abigael took out her phone and photographed the cattle who nudged the fence line to get close to the car. "I must send this to the rancher in Texas I visited last year. He will be fascinated."

The day waned as the car made its way to the farmhouse, set back on a hill overlooking the Tugela River. A large Zulu woman came out drying her hands on a bright apron and then stood with her hands on her hips as Bryan stopped the vehicle.

He jumped out and immediately threw his arms around this woman, whom he kissed soundly on the cheek. "Come Abigael and meet my aunt Mama Mary"

"Tsk Bryan, let the poor girl take her time. Her legs must be numb after your long drive. Come along child, I have a nice cold drink ready for you. Let Bryan bring in your luggage while we get to know each other. His parents are still out working on the farm. In fact, I am sure they heard the car and will have dropped everything to come and meet you." Mama Mary enveloped Abigael in a hug lifting her off her feet. Ushering a silent Abigael into a stunningly beautiful home of mud brick and thatch roof, she led the way to a sitting room decorated with a variety of artworks.

Abigael finally found her voice. "Mama Mary, it is so nice to meet you. This is marvelous. What a home." She wandered around, looking at the carved soap stone figures littering the surfaces and then the paintings depicting local scenery and wildlife. "Wow, this is fantastic. Who decorated this place because, seriously, my sister would be so envious of its beauty?"

Bryan walked in. "Mama Mary helped in the designs, but it is my mom who is the wizard with fabrics and furniture. This piece here came with her family from Singapore in the late 1800's and this here my parents bought when they went on a holiday to India three years ago." He touched a carved table and then a sideboard painted in bright shapes and colors as he walked towards them.

Mama Mary led the way into a kitchen with a huge coal-fired stove on one side and an electric equivalent on the other side. In the center was a plain wooden table showing signs of many meals and projects. A few knocks from a dropped utensil and a splash of blue paint spoke of happy hours spent around this communal gathering point. The chairs clustered around it were a hodgepodge of shapes and designs working to enhance the feeling of comfort and ease. Mama Mary brought bottles of ice-cold drinks from a large fridge, and she pointed at a cupboard. "Bryan, there are snacks in the cupboard. Bring them to the table. They should keep the wolves from the door until dinnertime."

You could see the love and respect between aunt and nephew as they worked in unison to set up the sparse meal. "What is your poison, Abigael? Tea, coffee, cocoa or maybe even a beer?" Mama Mary plopped herself down in the chair opposite her.

"Something cold would be great. But not beer. I have never taken to the taste and frankly, my parents did not encourage it either." Abigael replied.

Bryan walked over to the fridge and grabbed a can of beer for himself and a few glasses from a cabinet as he joined them both.

"Ginger beer. Or pineapple beer might be better than Abigael. My aunt is famous for both beverages and no, they are not alcoholic." He touched her leg underneath the table.

By the time his parents arrived ten minutes later, Bryan was grilled by his aunt about not coming home more often. He was desperately trying to defend his reasons and failing horribly. An older version of Bryan came through the door looking hot and bothered as he strode in.

"Hi, I am Stephen Bond; Bryan's father and you must be Abigael." He turned to Bryan. "Don't drink all my beers on your own. Get one for your old man. I am parched beyond belief." He shook Abigael's hand and then joined them at the table just in time to greet his wife.

Emma was nothing like Abigael imagined. First, she wore a pair of coveralls and second; she was tiny and blond and beautiful. Her smile lit up the room and she had a way about her of commanding the attention of all those present without saying a word. "No beer for me, Bryan. But I need a hug from my son. And then I will have a large glass of pineapple beer I have been craving all day."

She stood in front of Abigael and leaned down slightly to give her a hug. "Welcome to the family. Bryan tells me you are great with tools and all things mechanical. A woman after my heart," Folding her legs beneath her, she sat on the chair next to Abigael and leaned back. "So, tell me your side of the story. I don't know whether I can believe all my son has been telling me. He says it was love at first sight and the two of you are soul mates."

"Well, it's not quite accurate." Abigael announced and told them about the interview and how she never dreamed she would be chosen. She felt so comfortable with the family members and by the time the meal was prepared and served, it was she who helped Bryan set the table. They spent the evening getting to know each other and Abigael could see there was a camaraderie between father and son and a genuine love amongst them all.

Stephen stood up. "I am a farmer and as a farmer, I need to be up early. Sorry to leave you in the hands of my son, but I need my rest." He leaned over and gave Abigael a peck on her cheek. And the senior members of the family said their goodnights and left them on their own devices.

Abigael felt exhausted after her sleepless night and long drive and was not sure of what was expected of her. Bryan pulled her to her feet. "Mama Mary has prepared a chalet for you to sleep in, but I have my suite of rooms. You choose where you want to stay."

It felt natural and right to go with Bryan to his rooms and she was not surprised to see her luggage was already there. "You were confident I would choose this option, Bryan? Now, what if I decided not to join you tonight?"

"I would have brought your luggage over to your room, of course." He closed the door behind them. "The next few days are going to be hectic. How about we do actually sleep tonight and get our strength back."

But it was not quite as simple, because as Abigael dressed in the scandalous nightwear her sisters bought her, Bryan's eyes popped, and he observed the glimpses of her figure through the sheer fabric. "And here I thought you slept in t-shirts and shorts. How wrong could I have been?"

Their lovemaking was short and sweet before they both succumbed to slumber wrapped in each other's arms.

Morning brought with it a feeling of tranquility as Abigael woke to see Bryan watching her. Sunlight streamed through the window, and she heard the same bird she saw in Sun City. Eager to get dressed and start the day, she was detained by a hand on hers, dragging her back into bed. "Not so fast, sleeping beauty. Let me look at you a moment longer? Even with your hair all awry, you are stunningly beautiful." He ran his hand under her negligee and over her hips and upwards towards her breast. "Oh yes, beautiful doesn't do you justice. I am the luckiest man alive to wake up next to you for the rest of my life."

Unable to resist his charm or the touch of his hands, she straddled him as he lay supine on the bed. "Why do you love me, Bryan? I need to understand, because I can't see what you see." Abigael asked.

"Ah, well, let me see now. You are kind and intelligent. You love life and find simple things fascinating. And to top it all off, your figure is a marvel. Round where it needs to be round, and smooth and soft and oh, my goodness, I have never met a woman who is so honest and true. You have no guile. But most of all, you are the complement to my hardness. And no, I am not referring to what you think. Where I am all business, you find time to listen to others and care about their needs. And mine. You care about my needs." He smiled his bright smile up at her. "And why do you find me so loveable? I didn't exactly start this relationship on a romantic footing. Come on, I agree putting an advert in an engineering magazine is a bit strange?"

Abigael leaned over so her breasts brushed against his chest and her lips close to his ear. She said, "You see the real me, Bryan. You see me for who I can become, and I know you will encourage me to be the best person I can be." She nipped the lobe of his ear and then licked it lightly. "And you are so sexy in those blue jeans. Please say you will wear them every day for the rest of our lives. And as for the advert. I am grateful I applied for the position. I didn't think I would be chosen, but without it, we would never have met. And I am eternally grateful. Romance or not, it was perfect."

The morning sounds of the farm got louder through the window. She could hear a tractor starting up and a vehicle driving off. But when Bryan flipped her over to resume their lovemaking and declarations, she forgot everything except their needs and wants.

They were to drive to Durban to collect Abigael's two sisters later in the day and, after a quick shower and clean, they went to ask Mama Mary which rooms they should prepare for the visitors. They were given clean towels and sheets, scented soaps and small toiletries to place in the assigned quarters. The two of them got to work and were finished in plenty of time to get on the road to the airport.

Abigael wore her usual uniform of blouse and shorts and much to her delight, Bryan took her advice and wore his blue jeans as requested. The drive to the city was another new experience. High-rise buildings juxtaposed against a shimmering blue sea and sandy golden beaches. Itinerant traders set up stalls outside the airport building and the smells and sounds of Southern Africa were all around them as they parked.

They did not have long to wait before Zlotla and Rachel came through the arrivals lounge looking jet lagged and tired. Introductions made and Rachel gave a surreptitious thumbs up behind Bryan's back as he packed their luggage into the car. The two sisters immediately fell asleep in the comfortable back seat as they drove up the coast towards Bond's Drift town and through it towards the farm. Neither Bryan nor Abigael said a word as they travelled in case, they woke up the sleeping ladies. But they needn't have worried. Zlotla woke up as they slowed for the town center. "So, this is Africa?"

Bryan smiled over his shoulder. "Yes, deepest, darkest Africa, in all its glory. This town is where my ancestor, the original Stephen Bond, set up a business ferrying people across the Tugela River and into Zululand." He pointed out the window at the gathering of small businesses and buildings. "Not much to look at, but I am told a hundred and fifty years ago, it was the last taste of civilisation the Great White Hunters got to see before venturing into the unknown. We don't live in town anymore. My great-grandparents bought a small farm several years ago and my parents have developed it into a thriving business."

Much as the day before, it was Mama Mary who greeted the guests with her warm hugs and inviting nature. Abigael showed them to their room and Bryan said he would join his father on the farm for the afternoon.

"Wow Abigael. You struck it lucky. He is so gorgeous. Tall, dark and handsome and obviously madly in love with you." Rachel stated as he walked out of sight. "Have you showed off the nightwear we bought you? Was he impressed?"

Abigael blushed madly as she remembered the night before and the reaction to her negligee choice. "Yes, he appreciated your clothing taste Rachel." she giggled like a schoolgirl at the look of delight on her sisters' faces.

Zlotla lay her large suitcase on the bed and, with a flash of drama, opened it up to expose a stunningly beautiful wedding dress. Lace across the bodice and tiny cap sleeves and a flowing silky skirt looking perfect. As they stood staring at this creation, there was a knock on the door and

Emma Bond entered. "Oh. my goodness." She gasped. "How did you manage to buy a dress like this in the short time we gave you?"

"New York never sleeps. And I presume you are the mother of the groom?" Zlotla asked.

"Oops, sorry. Yes, let me introduce myself properly. I am Bryan's mother, Emma Bond. Call me Emma. No one calls me Mrs. Bond." She shook the two women's hands and then stood back to observe the marvel in the suitcase. "Do you have a veil? I have a mantilla I wore to my wedding. Yes, I know you are Jewish, but it would make me happy to see it worn again. It will bring back happy memories and go perfectly with this dress." She leaned forward to reverently touch the lace with a slightly shaking finger. "None of my daughters have worn it and I have been considering giving it away. Or maybe putting it in storage for the next generation?"

Rachel and Zlotla smiled and said in unison, "Perfect." They turned towards Abigael to see her reaction and found her with tears in her eyes.

"Thank you, Emma. I would be privileged to wear it. Jewish brides wear coverings on their heads, and it would be totally appropriate to use it." Abigael said through her tears.

The next few days saw Zlotla and Rachel confer with Mama Mary and Emma about food choices and the venue. No detail was forgotten. Flowers sourced and cakes baked. Bryan's little niece and nephew were to be in the bridal party, but apart from the close family, they would not be having many guests. Carl came with a date and Thandi was invited with Paris. Rosita, the girl who was at the original job interview, was now living in Namibia, tried to organise a flight to attend. Bryan's cousin. Terence was given the job of videotaping the nuptials so the family in the States could be part of the occasion.

Rosita hired a car in Durban and by lunchtime on the eve of the wedding, all the main guests were gathered. Paris was asked to join Kim's daughter and Rose's young son as the attendants. Rachel and Zlotla walked Abigael down the aisle, which was flanked by an avenue of pot plants leading to a garden pergola. Carl agreed to be the best man to stop arguments between Bryan's two brothers. The two brothers, Alan and Raymond, would accompany Abigael's sisters during the photo shoot. Kim and Rose were both very pregnant with their second children and Alan's wife. Teresa suffered morning sickness and she dashed for the loo at odd moments. So, the family happily planned the arrangements. They found an old set of stables which were altered into guest quarters and Emma and Mama Mary were kept busy cleaning them for the influx of visitors. Mama Mary's adoptive granddaughter arrived with mops and buckets to help and entertained them all with her amazing singing voice. The air fairly hummed with energy during the last hours of the day.

During the day, the local Sangoma arrived to throw the bones. Dressed in monkey skins and rattling shells, the old man set up in the middle of the lawn. Paris came running to tell them all to gather. And they hurried to the meeting place.

Peering through a headdress of strange design, the witch doctor waited patiently for his audience to make themselves comfortable. Bryan took Abigael's hand, and they sat down in front of the bag of sacred items. Bryan whispered the Sangoma was there to detect the spirits of the offended and malevolent entities. He used his thumbs to beat a small drum, first softly, then gaining in volume until he threw both hands in the air and allowed the silence to descend. Taking the dried bones in his hands, he shook them above his head, chanting and calling into the air. Bryan once again whispered softly, it was a great privilege to have this ceremony done for them. With a flourish, the Sangoma threw the bones in front of him. Holding his hands wide, he continued to chant until he was ready. Moving a bone to the side, he pronounced, "Zeyde, Zeyde do you give your blessing to this union?'

Abigael couldn't stop the shock from showing on her face as her grandfather's name was called.

"Zeyde is pleased. Now, let us cleanse the anger of the ancestors. Others are crowding in from a place far away in Europe. They have been hurt beyond what any person should be expected to endure. But today they are pleased to send down their love. Embrace the good and turn away from evil."

A few more bones were thrown, and incantations called to the four corners of the earth. Turning to Bryan, he smiled a toothless smile. "Today, the blood of your ancestors from time immemorial flows through your veins, and it sings within you. The love of the land, the care for the Nguni tribes and especially for future generations of you people, will be enhanced by your work with this woman by your side. You are thrice blessed." Rising from his seat, he gestured for Bryan and Abigael to join him. Taking a small pouch from his belt, he bade them bow their heads as he sprinkled the powder over them.

Abigael looked at Bryan with a query in her eyes. He answered softly, "Dried herbs and maybe some dried monkey dung." He said with a twinkle in his eye.

Abigael laughed softly, not sure if he was joking or not. The old man bowed to the gathered crowd and Mama Mary led him away to reward him with a meal for his troubles. Abigael saw him walking into the bush, leading a bleating goat on a string and a cage of live chickens carried by his assistants.

I do hope my sisters recorded it. She thought as she sat quietly and absorbed the strange experience. On the eve of the wedding, the women insisted Abigael sleep in a separate room from Bryan and told him to get lost and find something else to do as they prepared for the day ahead. Bryan, Carl and the rest of the male family members took off for town and an evening of revelry. But for Abigael, it was a much simpler night of being pampered. Rosita massaged her feet with fragrant oils and Zlotla buffed her fingernails. Rachel mixed up her favorite face mask of honey and oatmeal and applied it liberally. Mama Mary raided her vegetable garden for cucumbers to slice and add to the face masks. Emma and Thandi plied them all with food and drinks and they shared the stories of their own weddings and the attendant dramas.

"Well, as you may imagine, when I married Stephen, it was not the 'done' thing to have a cross-cultural marriage in South Africa. Stephen owned this bomb of a car, backfiring at the oddest times. We were sure we would be stopped along the way, but we were lucky and made the border with no issues. We drove to Swaziland and were married by an old priest in a chapel next to the casino. I wore a yellow sundress and, if I remember rightly, Stephen wore a pair of khaki shorts and a white shirt. Those were the best clothes we owned. When we returned to Bond's drift, his parents were so kind to us. They put on a special celebration to mark the occasion and his mother gave me the mantilla to wear. Mama Mary made me a simple white dress and I still have it hanging in my closet somewhere. And Stephen used his father's funeral suit for the vow and ring ceremony." She twisted the simple gold wedding band on her finger as she talked. "When the local constable became concerned and we were breaking apartheid laws, my father-in-law, Thomas, bought him an enormous bottle of brandy and all was well." Emma smiled at her memories. "We lived overseas for some years while Stephen competed in the surfing circuit. And when the children came along, there were more bottles of brandy delivered to the police station. The children all went to a private school because in those days, the Government schools were segregated. By the time our youngest, Raymond, started school, the laws changed, and apartheid was no more."

Kim said "Oh, I remember, Mom. We went to a Catholic church school and wore those awful hot and scratchy uniforms. One day, I stripped down to my undies and jumped in the fountain in front of the chapel. Mother Superior wasn't amused, and I was told to say my Hail Mary's. I didn't have a clue what a Hail Mary was in those days and to be truthful, I still have no clue."

Rose chipped in, "I was lucky. My siblings paved the way before me, and I think Mother Superior was pleased when I didn't get into the mischief my brothers did. And I always depended on you, Kim, to turn to for help."

"Oh yes, and our brothers threatened anyone who teased us. They promised they would dunk anyone who made fun of us in the Tugela River in full flood. It seemed to do the trick." Kim added.

Thandi attended a similar school and they compared notes as the evening wore on. Rose told of her wedding under a spreading baobab tree and Kim and Teresa told of the simple affairs their special days were. Zlotla and Rachel both kept quiet about their expensive and opulent weddings in New York.

The morning of the wedding arrived, and Abigael woke to a breakfast tray in bed. She could hear movement outside as tables and chairs were unloaded from a truck from the hire company. Mama Mary could be heard instructing them where to place them and it was Carl who knocked on her door a few moments later. "Morning ladies. The hairdresser has arrived and wants to know when she can come in and do her thing?"

Kim's husband, Jared, was about to take the photographs and it was him next who knocked on the door. "I thought we could do a few shots of you with your family before the wedding. My in-laws have this enormous mirror in their private lounge, and it would be ideal. Call me when you are ready."

Cramming the last of the poached egg into her mouth, and taking a gulp of orange juice, Abigael ran towards the shower. She dared not wait any longer in case someone else came calling. The hairdresser worked on her and chatted away about what a beautiful setting this was and how lucky she was. "Bryan is the most eligible bachelor in the area. I mean, what's not to love about him? Charm, gorgeous looks and lots of lovely money.

Yummy." She applied the hair dryer to the slowly drying curls. "Now there you are. You look gorgeous." She gave a final twist to a strand of hair.

"Did you say he's really rich? We have never discussed money and frankly, it is not important to either of us." Abigael said with a frown to the hairdresser as she packed up her tools.

"Oh yes, stinking rich. He is on the list of ten richest bachelors of Southern Africa. There will be a lot of envious girls out there ready to scratch out your eyes now he is getting married." She zipped up her bag. "I am surprised there is not a slew of journalists mugging you all for photos and the story of how you met?"

"Really? Mmm, a new wrinkle in the saga of Bryan Bond for you. He is a mystery." Abigael admitted as she bid the woman farewell.

Her sisters came to dress her in her wedding finery. And then Emma entered with the mantilla. She unpacked it from its tissue and laid it on the bed for the last inspection. "I have some pins for the hair to hold it in place." She unearthed an ornate box of glittering pins from her pocket. "And I have some orchids you can hold in your hands for the walk down the aisle." She dashed outside to collect the promised blooms.

Zlotla said, "I have a special gift from Grandma for you to carry with the orchids. It is a book of poems Grandpa gave her as their wedding gift when they got married. It is covered in white leather, and it is very special to Grandma, and it is her way of blessing this union." Zlotla took the small volume out of her own pocket as she revealed this family heirloom. "The poems are by Omar Khayyam, a Persian mathematician and are truly beautiful."

Abigael fought back the tears as she remembered her grandfather. "Thank you so much for bringing it with you, Zlotla. I will take great care of it."

Emma returned with some large moth orchids, still dripping with morning dew. They were cream in color and looked gorgeous against the lace of the mantilla. Emma carefully pinned them to Abigael's hair to hold the mantilla in place. Stepping back, she wiped away a tear. "You look so lovely. What a beautiful bride you are."

"Now you have something borrowed and something new. All we need is the something blue to complete the ensemble." Rachel suggested. With a flourish, she brought a lacy garter from behind her back with tiny blue flowers embroidered around the elasticised center. "Put out your leg, Abigael, and I will make sure it is in the right position for your husband to remove once you are married."

With these special women making sure all the traditions were covered, Abigael stood in front of the mirror and twirled around. She hardly recognised herself in all her finery. "Time to find Jared and his camera." Emma suggested as she handed out white parasols to the women. "This is to protect Abigael from view in case Bryan peeps out of his room. We need to make sure she is not seen when she walks into the house. It is bad luck for the groom to see the bride before the wedding. I know it is a silly tradition, but who cares? Come along, women, let's snap to it."

Emma and Stephen's private lounge with walls of pale blue silk embossed with faded gold patterns embossed on it. Abigael gasped at the beauty of the room. The Italian style furniture suited Emma to a tee, but for the life of her, Abigael could not imagine Stephen being comfortable in this room. The large gold-framed mirror took up almost one entire wall and must have taken an engineer to ensure it remained on the wall safely. But none of the other women seemed impressed with this feat of skill and were focused on making sure Abigael was seated in the perfect spot. First, the three sisters were positioned and then Emma joined Abigael and finally the three children were brought in, dressed in their finery. Jared adjusted the lighting and moved the furniture until he was pleased with the compositions. "I usually photograph animals who are not keen to be placed perfectly for the shot. So, this is fun. A small smile, Abigael. Mmm and then look at me through your eyelashes. Yes. It's the money shot. Maybe I should make this into a calendar for you to give to all your friends and family who can't be here?" He mused as he tweaked the dress and then the mantilla one last time.

But it was time for the wedding ceremony. In honor of the Jewish tradition of not getting married on Saturday, they chose Friday to get wed. As Abigael stood at the entrance to the aisle of plants, she felt a twinge of regret her parents were not walking with her. She grasped her sisters' hands as she waited for the call to move forth. And then she heard a familiar call which heralded her sister's weddings. The three children threw rose petals in front of her as she walked towards Bryan. All she could focus on was his big smile and the tears in his eyes as he observed her.

Rachel and Zlotla handed her over to Bryan and then took their seats. "Today we will offer a blessing on the bride and groom." Uncle Daniel intoned. "After we have read a few words from the Torah in honor of the bride."

Abigael's head came up in surprise at this turn of events. She didn't know this was about to take place. And there, in front of her, under a canopy of a silken sheath of fabric, was a copy of the scriptures laying on a cushion. She turned slightly to look at her sisters and noticed their silly grins of delight at the surprise.

Uncle Daniel performed the ceremony perfectly and even asked Bryan to sign a contract of responsibilities before he could proceed.

Finally, they exchanged rings and then it was the turn of seven friends and family members

to read out the blessings. "I bless you with
health." Carl intoned.

"I bless you with happiness." Alan
followed.

"I bless you with peace." Kim said.

Until finally, the family and friends having
said their piece and it was time to seal their union
with the broken glass. Abigael recognised a glass
from her own parents' cabinet and the tears
gushed out of her eyes as she regretted their
absence. She knew they did not enjoy travelling
and grandma was in no state to go anywhere. She
wanted them there close to her in her moment of
joy.

The cloth it was wrapped in was a silk
scarf she was sure she saw yesterday in Emma's
lounge.

"With this breaking of the glass, we
symbolise what God has joined, let no man
destroy. Marriage is full of pain, but we can
overcome the challenges with perseverance. Now,
guests, Bryan and Abigael, will spend a few
minutes on their own considering the vows they
have made. You may all offer your congratulations
later when we will dance their good fortune in
finding each other in this world of toil and strife."
Uncle Daniel concluded as Bryan turned to
Abigael and, for the first time, they had a moment
together without distractions. He took her hand in
his and led her down towards a beautifully
decorated table, set with a simple meal.

"Abigael, wife, lover and my friend, how did you enjoy your special day? Your sisters were amazing. They planned everthing down to the most minor details and poor Uncle Daniel was schooled in the correct way to marry us." He leaned forward and kissed away her tears as she shook her head.

"Bryan, I really thought I wouldn't care about my family traditions, but I was wrong. It was beautiful." Abigael placed the volume of poems and her orchids on the table as she turned to her new husband and fell into his arms. With her face pressed to his chest, she said, "What have I done to deserve this? It was perfect."

Swaying slightly, Bryan hugged her to him as they sat quietly for a moment. She got up from her seat and moved to his lap so they could be closer. "This book belonged to my grandfather, and he gave it to my grandmother when they married. Do you want me to read you one poem?"

Nodding his head in agreement, he listened as she intoned the poem; she remembered her grandfather reciting to her over the years. "All I need, my love, is a loaf of bread and a jug of wine." She laughed at the look of shock on Bryan's face. "Yup, his favorite quote. He thought it epitomised his view of life. Actually, the correct quote is a book of verses under the bough, a jug of wine and thou beside me singing in the wilderness. Oh, wilderness was paradise enow." Kissing him lightly on the nose, she said, "I will sing with you in the wilderness, and it will be paradise. I promise."

Bryan said, "And now I wish I took more interest in poetry at school. I remember something, though it might not be romantic. It is from Lewis Carroll. The Walrus and the Carpenter were walking close to hand; They wept like anything to see, such quantities of sand: If this were only cleared away, they said, 'It would be grand.'" Bryan smiled into Abigael's eyes. "Maybe I should re-write it for us? The Engineer and the philanthropist were walking close at hand; They wept like anything to see, the inequality of the land: If this were only cleared away, they said, it would be more than grand."

Abigael kissed him and whispered. "A poet at heart. And a man with more care and concern for the underdog than I have ever met before. Together we will make beautiful music, lift the poor and needy and inspire the rich and powerful."

"Oh yes, how true. I haven't bought you a wedding gift for Abigael. The only gift I offer is my promise to be faithful and true. I know it is not much, but I will make it up to you over the years, if I can."

"My gift to you is almost as expensive." Abigael laughed. "It is my promise to be all the things I might be to you. And if I fall short, then I will try harder and hope you can help me along the way."

"We will help each other, Abigael. Always and forever."

It was time for them to return to their guests and Abigael made sure the book of poems was safely tucked away in Bryan's pocket.

Both cultures were happily embraced. The garter was thrown to the unmarried men, which comprised of Raymond and Carl and the orchids were placed on the grave of Bryan's grandparents in the family cemetery. A cake baked by Mama Mary was cut and distributed by the pregnant ladies in the family. And then it was time for Abigael to change out of her beautiful dress and into something a bit more practical.

When they returned to the gathering, there was one last gift to be given. Stephen led them all to the cattle pen. "The bride price for a woman of purity is many cattle. Today, we honor this tradition by gifting these two beasts to the family of the bride. The bull is of great heritage and lineage, as is his cow." He turned to Zlotla. "Now they belong to you. I know they are difficult to pack into a suitcase, so I will care for them on your behalf and if your parents ever come for a visit, I hope they will have produced many more cows for the wealth of your family."

Zlotla and Rachel were dumbstruck at this strange tradition and shrugged in confusion. Bryan whispered, "It is customary for you to thank my father for his generosity. The more you praise the cattle, the better he will like it."

Rachel stepped forward. "Oh, great chief of the tribe of Bond, we honor your bride price for this worthless child of my parent's loins. You are gracious and generous, and we are overwhelmed by your offer. Today we thank you on behalf of our parents. Tomorrow we will consult with them what should be done to recompense you for these beautiful creatures taking our breath away … and…" Rachel seemed to stumble as she sought for words.

Zlotla took over the oration with her own flair. "The Rabinowitz family thank you and in reply we will gift a scholarship for a worthy student in your name here in Zululand. We will offer a placement at an Ivy league university in America if it's where they wish to study. Or at a British university at our own personal expense. My parents are happy to take part in your established scholarship program and enhance it where we can." She bowed towards Stephen and Emma as she concluded her own offering.

Hands were shaken and cheeks kissed as they discussed the ramifications of these dealings. During this exchange, Bryan and Abigael quietly left and drove off into the Mercedes Benz. No one seemed to notice their departure and it was only later they complained about the chance to give them a proper sendoff.

The wedding took almost all day and as Bryan and Abigael drove down the highway; she did not know where they were heading. Bryan put on some music to fill the air with cheerful sounds and Abigael sang along to the songs she knew. Bryan tapped his fingers on the steering wheel along with the beat. Abigael saw a sign announcing they were arriving at Umhlanga Rocks and then she glimpsed the sea glittering in the fading light. She cracked the window and could smell the ozone as it wafted towards her.

"We are almost home, sweetheart. Not far now." Bryan announced.

As they turned into a driveway, Bryan pushed a button opening a large garage door. The lights came on automatically and the door closed behind them. Abigael went to open her door, but Bryan put his hand out. "One last tradition to fulfil before the day ends."

Jumping out, he came around and opened her door and then leaned in and lifted her into his arms. "I am told I should carry you over the threshold of our home. So, come along, Mrs. Bond, relax and let me finish my duties for the day." Striding towards a bright blue door, he deftly opened the lock with a keypad and a twist of the handle. "Welcome to our home."

Abigael could immediately sense Mama Mary and Emma's hands in decorating the home, as interesting pieces of furniture and bright materials abounded. She looked up and past the lounge suite to be surprised at a view of the sea. She could hear the crashing waves and turned to Bryan. "Is this your home? How beautiful. I thought you lived in a camp all the year around."

"Oh no. Summer is much too hot for camp life. So, each year, just before Christmas, we pack up and have our down time. We spend three months doing fund raising, looking for new projects and sometimes we even have a few days lying around the pool. This is my summer home and now it is yours, too." Bryan admitted as he placed her on her feet in the middle of a pale blue Persian rug. "Here is where I come to be indulgent and lazy and totally at peace. This year we went to America for a month, where we met you. Then a month of fund raising and this last month, I am dedicating to you and me." He led her out to a deck overlooking the ocean and a small swimming pool on a lower level. "We have another ten days here and then will need to return to the Makatini flats to prepare for the influx of volunteers."

Standing behind her, he said, "Look over there. A school of dolphins has come to welcome you to this place. Sometimes we get whales breaching, but perhaps not at this time of the year so much." He pulled her close to his chest. "Now, let me show you the rest of the house."

Abigael felt his pride at showing her his abode and she took his hand happily as he led her through the home. She could be at peace here. This could be her safe place, too. Smiling happily as he finally led her into the main bedroom suite, she stopped at the door and gasped. There on the bedside table were photographs of her family in silver frames. There was even one of her grandfather's smiling at her. Turning to Bryan.

"How?" was all she could get out of her mouth.

"Your sisters sent a file I printed up. My housekeeper bought the frames and set them up for you. I hope you like them. Jessica has superb taste, and I trusted her to do things right."

"They are perfect" She felt the tears streaming down her cheeks and she touched each photo with love. She even felt happy to see a photo of Joseph amongst the group.

"No more tears, sweetheart. This is supposed to be the happiest day of your life." Bryan encouraged her.

"It is Bryan, it is." Abigael took his hand and pulled him down on the bed with her. "No more tears. Let's try out the mattress. Oh, and I love the bedding. So, gorgeous." She allowed her fingers to touch the different cushions.

"Well, we can't have the bedding being the star of the piece. Let me collect your luggage and I will meet you here in five minutes. And you better not be loving the duvet cover more than me. I am a jealous man, you know." Bryan laughed at this statement and strode out of the room, leaving Abigael to spend a moment taking it all in.

The crisp white spread on the bed and the earthy toned accents perfectly matched what she would have chosen for herself. There was a large mirror on the wall reminding her of Emma's lounge at Bond's drift. She stared at herself for a moment and hardly recognised the woman looking back at her. There was a confidence in her eyes she always knew was there, but now it was clear. Is this what the love of a good man did for her? Instead of judging her figure against the models in magazines, she smiled as she ran her hands over her hips in pleasure. Bryan walked in to find her standing in her underwear, observing herself with her head tilted to the side.

"Now, this I can get used to. Come here, Mrs. Bond, and let me help you divest yourself of these earthly restraints." Bryan stood behind her in the mirror as he slowly removed the garments until she stood naked in front of him. "I have never made love to a married woman before. I am just wondering if it is something different. Will I feel naughty or nice?" He mused as he kissed her neck and, as the sun set, he led her to the bed.

The night was almost as frenetic as the first night they made love. They barely slept between discovering what the other person enjoyed. At midnight, they went for a swim in the pool. Naked as jaybirds, they let the water soothe their heated bodies. They ate cheese toasties at two o'clock in the morning and pancakes and honey and fresh strawberries for breakfast. Their lovemaking seemed to make them hungry, not only for each other, but for the pleasures of food and all its delights. They laid around the pool during the morning wearing only sunshades and sunscreen. The afternoon they watched a movie on the large television in the lounge wearing absolutely nothing at all. In fact, Bryan paused the movie at one stage as the urge for more love making overtook them. Jessica, the housekeeper, left the freezer well stocked with pre-prepared meals and they reheated a meal as the sunset once more. They slept for a while in the evening and then took a bath in the tub which turned into something much more enjoyable than just getting clean.

The dawn saw Abigael bleary eyed and aching throughout her body. She'd used muscles and felt things she never imagined. Bryan brought her a cup of coffee as he sat on the corner of the bed. "Sweetheart, Jessica is coming in today. We will need to get dressed before she arrives. And, I must go into town for a meeting with the Norwegian ambassador about funding a project we have planned. Carl and I will be busy all day and again tomorrow with some other investors. You relax and I will see you later." Bryan leaned down and kissed her on her nose as he stood up and walked out.

"I suppose the honeymoon is finished, then?"

"Not if I have anything to say about it. Two days, sweetheart. And then it will be just you and me. I promise." Bryan sighed softly. "I will count the minutes and wish I were back here with you."

She heard the garage door open, and the car drove away as she considered what she would do. They passed a set of shops on their way here, but it was now Sunday, and she did not know if they would be open. But at least she could go for a walk, she thought. She was sitting on the lounger on the front patio reading a novel when she heard a woman call out, "Cooee, it's me, Jessica."

Abigael stood up and went into the house to meet the woman who took such care to present her family photos for her. Jessica was a large woman who was unpacking a bag of groceries onto the kitchen countertop.

"Hi Jessica, I am Abigael. It is so nice to meet the person who takes such good care of this home." Abigael and Jessica spent a few minutes introducing themselves.

Switching on the electric kettle, Jessica said, "Let's sit and chat for a while."

But as she said this, there was a knock on the front door.

"Now who could it be?" Jessica asked with a smile on her face and a twinkle in her eyes as if she already knew the answer.

Zlotla was the first to enter and rushed over to give Abigael a hug. "Your new husband said you might be lonely today because of his business meetings. And so, he invited us to join your honeymoon." She laughed to see the genuine surprise on Abigael's face. "Well, now we know he can keep a secret." She stated.

Rachel pulled their suitcases behind her as she joined them all in the kitchen. Jessica put out four mugs and was busy at a very fancy coffee machine at the counter.

Within minutes of greeting her sisters, Jessica placed steaming hot cups of coffee in front of them all and was ferreting in the cupboard for a container of home-made cookies.

"Now we can get to know each other better." Jessica lowered her colossal frame into a chair. "Bryan said his wife's sisters would join us today for a two-day visit. I have made up the two bedrooms on the lower level for you to use. After coffee, I will take you to your rooms." She huffed slightly as she took a sip of her own brew and reached for a cookie to dunk.

They happily chatted away about the beauty of the setting, and Jessica filled them in on its history. "Bryan bought an empty piece of land about ten years ago. Then he and Carl cleared it of all the bushes and snakes by hand. I live across the road and could see those two poor men sweating like navies long into the night. One day I came over with a meal for them and it was the beginning of a great friendship. They pay me well, and I hope I return the favor by working hard. Carl has a house next door and I work two days a week for him and two days for Bryan." She ran her hand over the wood of her chair. "First Carl and Bryan lived on site in a tent, but they were hard at work to set down foundations for these lovely homes they have created."

Finishing her drink, she levered herself up. "Come along ladies, the downstairs awaits you." Taking one suitcase in hand, she led the way. Abigael hadn't looked at the lower level and happily followed along on this voyage of discovery. The two bedrooms, both with small patios and large bathrooms, were as good as any which graced a five-star hotel in any country in the world.

Each room was identical, and both were gorgeously appointed. Large king-sized beds covered in duvets and throws, one in a floral theme and the other in shades of the seashore. Paintings adorned the walls and looked like they were original and not prints. "Nothing but the best for our Mister Bond." Jessica admitted as she smoothed down one of the soft woolen throws. She smiled at Abigael as she said this.

When Bryan returned from his business meeting, he brought Carl with him and took them all out to dinner at Olive and Oil, a local restaurant. Zlotla and Rachel seemed to be having a great time and Abigael was pleased to see them enjoying their mini holiday. They showed Carl and Bryan photos of their children and their husbands and laughed at the thought of Sara trying to look after the school runs for their various needs.

Rachel said, "Sara has been talking about having another child. A week with my bunch will change her mind for good. They are a handful." The look of pride and love on her face was at odds with her words and Abigael knew she was eager to return to the madness of her life.

Zlotla's children ranged from one-year-old to ten and she too showed off her family with pride and a hint of sadness for having missed a school play because of this trip clashing with the well-planned schedule.

Both women spent the rest of the evening on their phones, chatting to their husbands and children halfway across the world.

The following day, the women went shopping in the mall and Zlotla bought some interesting bead work she hoped to import and sell in America. It was rare the three sisters could relax in the sun together. And sunny it was. The temperature hovering around the "too hot to move" heat and they found the coolness of the air-conditioned shops much more to their liking. Abigael found a small second-hand bookstore in the mall and asked about the Rudyard Kipling books she promised to buy for Paris. There were none in stock, but the shop owner was keen to source some for her and said she would deliver them in person once they arrived. The surname of Bond obviously opened doors not offered to Miss Abigael Rabinowitz.

The two sisters were catching an early flight the following morning and it was with sadness they linked arms and strolled back to the house. "Thank you for joining me on my honeymoon, guys. It will certainly be something to tell the grandkids one day when I am old and gray." Abigael laughed.

She could still not believe this fairytale life
was hers. Less than two months ago, she thought
her life would be one of drudgery and boredom
caring for her parents until the day they died. As
Bryan walked through the door, she could not
help smiling with joy. Life turned out to be all she
could ever wish for, and she hoped it would never
change.

She snuggled into Bryan as evening fell,
with a feeling of love and contentment in her
heart.

The next few days flew by in a flash of
passion and excitement as they found joy in each
other. There were days when they never left the
house and others where they went exploring along
the shore. Searching for exotic shells in crystal
clear rock pools and swimming in sheltered coves
with only the dolphins and monkeys for company.
But it could not last forever and the day they
returned to Makatini, Abigael knew her
honeymoon was perfect.

The final few miles to the camp were
spent in silence as they thought about the next few
days. The volunteer tourists would only arrive in
ten days' time, but there was plenty to keep them
busy in the meantime. Thandi sent over a few
helpers to clean up the hammock dormitories and
Carl was busy checking the tools and the
equipment. Bryan spent the first day back down at
the dam, pacing up and down, measuring depths
and distances. Abigael was back in her usual

uniform of shorts and shirts and strode alongside him as he mumbled his thoughts aloud. "Still not deep enough over here. Is the soil too porous? Will it all leak away when the rains are finished?"

Each concern saw him frowning with concentration. Abigael went back to the camp and left him to work through the problems while she made sure there were enough food stocks to feed a dozen hungry students. She stepped into the workshop area when she was finished and sat down at the computer to send off a message to her family. Carl was working through the things they would need and the tasks they could ask students to complete.

"We have three engineering students from Norway, and they should be great. But I am not sure about this group from Sweden? Anthropologists. Well, they should have plenty to keep them busy. I know one of them is a doctorate student and has asked if he can interview the indigenous tribesmen. Hah. Let's hope it goes down well with Thandi." Carl sat on the edge of the desk as he looked at his clipboard. "Then we have five Americans who want to be of service to the poor. Well, we can only hope they don't stuff things up too badly. At least they will have you to turn to for advice if they make a mess of their time here."

He put the clipboard down. "We often get people to arrive here with romantic ideas of what they will be doing. It usually takes a week of two to knock off their rough edges and get them to appreciate the ancient way the of Zulu hierarchy and traditions and work for the general good."

Abigael looked up at him. "Am I like those romantic Americans, Carl?"

"Oh Abigael, you are a whole different kettle of fish. You are strange and unusual and the perfect match for my friend." Carl laughed at the look on Abigael's face. "No, you are not the usual sort of American. We get volunteering. We have some who want to shoot the Big Five animals of Africa. With guns, not cameras. Which we do not allow, of course. We have others who have a Santa Claus mentality and want to hand out charity by the bucket load. And we get the bleeding hearts who think they can change the world by loving everyone. You will meet them all."

Bryan strode up the steps. "What's going on here?"

"I am telling Abigael about the students we have arriving in a few days' time and what to expect. Should we put her on gun patrol? She can inspect their bags to make sure none of them are packing automatic rifles. Although, how they would have got them past security at the airport is anyone's guess."

Bryan put his arm around Abigael's shoulders. "Nope, let us not scare her away so early on the piece. We can have her working with the engineering students and keep them on track." He pulled out the worksheet for the next few weeks and laid it in front of Abigael. "We start them on simple tasks like laying pipes or digging holes for supports. Nothing too strenuous and nothing too scary in the first week. It's why we are so successful at what we do. We lead them slowly down to hell, one step at a time." He laughed at his own turn of phrase and both Carl and Abigael joined him in his laughter.

Thandi and Paris joined them after dinner and Abigael could hand over her gift of books to the young child. While Thandi and the men sat huddled around the names of the volunteers and their particular skills, Abigael read the first story to Paris in the light of a string of fairy lights strung between the trees. The book was quite old and on its cover was a picture of an elephant in a river with an enormous snake slithering through the water.

"Which story do you want first, Paris? How the whale got into his throat? Or, How the leopard got its spots? You can choose whichever one you want." Abigael looked up to see Bryan smiling at her across the table.

Paris was thumbing through the book. "This one is about the butterfly. Please, Abigael, read it to me."

"Sure, it is about a butterfly who wanted to stamp its feet. It is my favorite too. It has people from my scriptures in the story. There is King Solomon and how the Queen of Sheba, or Balkis, used this story to stop his wives from scolding him." Abigael opened the book to the correct page and started reading. For each character, she changed her voice subtly and Paris was not her only listener. The other adults stopped talking and all leaned forward to hear the saga of the butterfly.

"Now King Solomon married many wives, but the one he loved the most was Balkis. One day, the king was walking through the forest he came across two butterflies arguing. The Daddy butterfly said if he stamped his foot, the huge palace garden would disappear. While the king speaks to the Daddy butterfly and promises to help him, Balkis is talking to the Mommy butterfly. She suggests the Mommy challenge the Daddy to stamp his foot and then see what happens. Okay, now let us read the story as Rudyard Kipling wrote it."

By the end of the story, Paris was fast asleep, and Carl offered to carry her home to her bed. Bryan took Abigael by the hand. "Will you tell me a bed-time story too my wife? I promise not to threaten to stamp my feet."

Laughing at his reference to the story, Abigael stood up and went straight into his arms. She felt the thrill of touching him rush through her body and whispered. "I have something much more fun to do than read a book, my dear husband."

They didn't hear Carl return, but an hour later, they were lying entwined in each other's arms and heard a distant sound, which caused Bryan to sit up straight in bed. "Gunfire Abigael. And it sounds like it is from Thandi's village." He frantically pulled on jeans and shoes as the noise continued.

The pop pop of noise was nothing like Abigael heard in movies, but she knew Bryan was telling the truth by the look on his face. Their bedroom door was ripped open as Carl rushed in. He threw a gun towards Bryan. "Hurry. They don't sound like friendlies."

"Abigael, I will send out the children if it is safe. Take them to the dam and hide. I trust you with their welfare. Stay safe, sweetheart. Stay safe." Bryan dropped a quick peck on her cheek before thrusting a pistol into her hands. "I should have given you lessons on how to use it. Do your best and don't shoot me or any of our friends."

With this admonition ringing in her ears, Abigael found her own clothes and dressed in the dark. She was scared to go out into the night and told herself there was no other option. "Now is the time for all brave men and women to step up to the plate." She said to herself as she pushed the pistol into her waistband and stepped outside.

The fairy-lights usually adorning the trees in the camp were extinguished and it took a moment for her eyes to adjust to the light of the stars in the sky. There was no moon, and it was almost impossible to see further than a few feet in front of her. She heard a rustle near the gate and her heart leapt in her throat. "Who is it?" She whispered.

"It's me, Abigael. Me and my grandmother and my cousins. Bryan said you would come with us to safety." Paris was dressed in a bright pink dressing gown and seemed to be covered with unicorns. But Abigael was not sure, and she didn't really care, as long as the children were out of the gunfight.

She was not sure if it was Paris leading the way to safety, or grandmother or even herself. They all seemed to know what the plan was, and Abigael was happy to follow along. She picked up a small child who struggled to keep up and looked over to see the grandmother with another child strapped to her back and two more holding her hands. Even young Paris carried a child in her arms. She was staggering valiantly along the track. One of the young boys walked behind them with a branch and tried his best to wipe out their tracks as best he could. None of the children made a sound. All of them knew the consequences of alerting the attackers to their position. Even the baby on Grandmother's back was silent.

As they walked, the sound of gunfire continued in the still night. A new sound heralded the use of a Kalashnikov. Paris whispered the answers to her unasked questions before she could give them a voice. "AR 15, it has a distinctive sound. And the other sound is an AK 47 or Kalashnikov. The little pop is a pistol, and my aunts use those for close up shooting." She adjusted her little cousin on her hip and then said, "My Mom has an AR 15 and Bryan and Carl too. So, the AK 47 must be the bad guys." There was the slightest quaver in her voice as she spoke.

Grandma walked up closer. "We must find somewhere the children can rest and then I will run to the next village and get help. You need to stay with the little ones while I am gone and try to keep them quiet." In the dark, there was no way to see if Grandma was afraid. Her voice wavered slightly, but Abigael couldn't fault her on such a small sign of fear. Her knees shook and she bit down on her lip to stop herself from keening with distress.

They reached the dam and Grandma looked around for a good hiding spot. "Over here. This is where they have started the pumping station. Behind here are some low bushes. The little ones can lie down on the sand and the older ones keep watch."

Abigael was in awe of the old lady's eyesight in this dim light but did not question her wisdom. "The evil men will hurt the children if they find us. Or they might use them as leverage to get what they want from my daughter. Thandi is strong, but even she has her limits and one of those is her daughter's well-being." She patted Abigael on the shoulder and then melted into the night so silently she walked right past a small gecko without waking it up.

The boy tasked with brushing away their footsteps, hunkered down next to Abigael and Paris. "I am Jafari. Can you tell me if you can see any of our marks in the sand?" He sounded scared and Abigael was not surprised.

She lifted a branch to allow him access to their hideaway. "You have done an excellent job, Jafari. I can't see a mark."

Some children fell asleep as if oblivious to the drama being played out in their village. The older children were not so at ease. Each child cuddled up to each other for comfort. In her rush to get dressed, Abigael put on her clothes from the day before and there was a packet of sweeties she bought in town still in her pocket. Taking them out, she handed one each to the children.

Paris whispered, "Abigael, can you tell us all a story, so we do not think of the wicked men and the fight?"

"Sure Paris. Let me tell you about the crocodile. I will have to remember it because we didn't bring the book with us." Abigael tried to remember the best she could.

The night moved forward on leaden wings. The stars moved and the stories came. Children woke and wanted food or drink and Abigael did her best to meet their needs when all she really wanted to do was run and see if Bryan was still alive. Was this her true love and would she lose him to a bullet? The sweat on her brow dripped down and joined the tears finding their way out of her eyes. She was thankful the children could not see them and all she could do was wait. Grandma returned as the sun rose and she scuttled into their refuge.

"The people of the other village do not have many weapons. But they will do what they can to help. They are skilled hunters and many of them can kill an antelope on the run but have never fought off the two-legged jackals before." She referred to the ubiquitous poachers of the area. "There are a few men left in our villages. They go to the gold mines and the cities to find work to support the families left behind. Even the older teenagers are away at boarding schools or finding work where they can." She sighed. "But we will do the best we can with what we have."

She sank to the ground and Abigael handed her a sweetie in silence as she noted the weary droop of the old lady's shoulders.

"We have heard no noise for the past hour, Gogo. Maybe they have given up and left?" She added hopefully, using the familiar name for grandmother in the moment of relief.

And then Jafari touched her silently on the arm, and she stopped speaking. Coming into the clearing in the early morning light was a man with his head down, searching the ground for prints. He stopped where a grass stem lay broken and then hunkered down to look at the path at an oblique angle.

Abigael quietly took the pistol from her belt and checked to see if the safety was on. She had never fired a gun in anger in her life but played paintball with a few friends over the years and knew the basics. She never took her eyes off the man as he inched forward, one step at a time. Abigael was surprised to see he was Asian and wondered what brought him to Africa and especially to their corner of Africa. Paris whispered in her ear. "I know him. He came with those Chinese businessmen who wanted to buy our land."

Well, one question about how they knew where to come, and where to attack, was answered. One baby stirred and Grandma quickly took the sweetie out of her own mouth and placed it in the child's mouth to keep it quiet. The tension in the air was palpable as the Asian man searched the area. It was only a matter of time before their hiding place would be discovered and then what would they do? Would she be brave enough to shoot this man? She could only hope so.

Suddenly, he was lying face down in the dust with a spear sticking out of his back. Grandma grunted in surprise. "I recognise the spear. It belongs to my nephew, but he is away working in the mines. So, who threw it with such accuracy?"

Her queries did not have long to be answered as a young woman came forward from her concealment to inspect her handiwork. "Gogo. You can come out now. There is no one else on the path."

Jafari and this young woman hid the body under a pile of earth, using the discarded shovels left behind from digging the dam. Grandma went on her way to the other village with the children in tow. Abigael knew she could not go with them. Her heart was calling for her to find Bryan. Paris followed her grandmother, but Jafari and the young woman turned to Abigael. "Come with us. We can take you safely there to the village of Thandi."

The going was slow. Each step taken, a master class in concealment. Jafari and Amahle, the girl, were so stealthily, at times Abigael lost sight of them even though she was only one step behind. At one stage, Amahle stopped and stooped over a muddy puddle. She smeared the mud over Abigael's face and arms. "You are too white. They will see you." Then she splashed the mud all over Abigael's pale-yellow blouse. "You must appear like a bush. When they look right at you, they should think you are a branch and not a person."

She looked at Abigael's shoes and nodded. "The shoes have soft soles but try not to kick a stone or a rock. Our lives depend on it." She retrieved her father's spear from the back of the tracker and was now eager to find a new target.

As they got closer to the village, they slowed down even more. Jafari climbed a thorn tree to see if he could find out the position of the enemy. With hand signals his cousin understood, but Abigael could not, he gestured towards an area behind the cattle kraal. When he returned to the ground, Amahle changed direction, so they circled around the village and approached from the opposite side and closest to the cattle pen.

Abigael gasped as she saw a body lying in a pool of blood. A young boy who herded the cows on guard duty against predators did not see the knife slitting his throat. He stared up sightlessly at the dawn. Moving through the cattle, Jafari and Amahle kept them quiet with a gentle touch of the hand and they could reach the brush wall closest to the village with no alarm being set off. Peering through the thorn branches, Abigael saw about ten men gathered around a large vehicle. Sitting on the hood of their truck was a man holding an AK 47 across his knees. In the vehicle's shade, Abigael saw Bryan, Carl and Thandi tied up like hogs ready for the slaughter. Bryan sported a nasty cut on his head and blood was dripping down onto his shirt. Carl was shot in the leg and a makeshift bandage oozing blood into the dirtcovered the wound . It was only Thandi who seemed unhurt. Abigael's heart sank. She hoped the men would prevail against the invaders, but it was not so.

Thandi sat with a defiant look on her face as a Chinese man in a suit paced up and down in front of her. Their conversation was clear in the morning air and the three would be rescuers could hear every word being said.

"Sign the papers, woman. Do you want us to kill your whole family for a piece of earth? Do not think I will not kill you, too. There is always someone more accommodating in the tribe happy to take our money. Now sign."

Thandi, with tears streaming down her cheeks as she answered. "Never. This land belongs to my people, and you want to mine it? Never. Not for all the gold in China." She clenched her jaws and lifted her chin in defiance.

"We have trackers out looking for your family. With your pretty little daughter in our clutches, we will see how you change your mind." He spat in the dust and sighed deeply. As if disgusted at this turn of events, the man walked to the back of the truck and climbed inside.

Amahle and Jafari signaled they were leaving, but Abigael refused to go. Bryan was so close she could almost touch him and there was no way she would want to be anywhere else at this moment. The two youngsters vanished between the legs of the cattle and left Abigael watching the proceedings in the village. She knew there was no chance of killing a man who was holding an AK 47, but she could dream. Abigael wondered how many of the tribe escaped into the safety of hiding places and how many were lying injured in the bush? Hopefully, the people from the neighboring village would take care of them. And then she saw Bryan lift his head slightly and look directly at her hiding place. He lifted his chin as if to say she should leave and she shook her head in denial, hoping he could see her movement. He was whispering something to Thandi as he watched, and Abigael saw the chieftain lift her head and raise her eyebrows in query. Abigael hunkered down as she watched her friends and her husband, helpless and hurt. Carl did not look well and groaned as he tried to get comfortable. But with their hands tied behind their backs, it was an arduous task.

The sun rose and the Chinese businessman returned. In his hand he held a mug, which, from the aroma wafting across the space, was obviously some sort of tea. "Have you thought about my offer, Miss Khumalo? Your time is running out. I will need your signature by the end of the day or else I will take further steps to get your compliance."

This time, Thandi did not raise her head and sat there as if she were deaf to his threats. "Sundown. You have until the sun sinks below the horizon and then I will kill your friends if they are not already dead by then." He kicked Carl in his injured leg and Abigael saw him flinch in pain.

Abigael felt a tap on her ankle and turned to see Jafari return with a calabash of water for her to drink. He put his lips close to her ear. "The tribe is gathering, and we have a plan to save our chieftain. Do not fear. Keep your head low."

Abigael whispered in his ear and told him of the threats uttered by the Chinese businessman. "Sundown. We only have till sundown." She knew he could hear the fear in her words but did not care. "Are the evil men at our camp? Perhaps there is something there which can help us?"

Jafari nodded his head and then, like a wisp of smoke, vanished once more between the cattle. The cows became restless in their confined space and finally the guard with the gun called out to his boss.

"Those beasts must be released to eat and drink, boss. Can I let them out?"

"Darren, do what you like with the animals. I really don't care. But take Mister Bond and Chi with you. They can do the work while you keep watch. Zhu has not come back from his tracking assignment, and I don't want to lose any more men to this wild land." The Chinese businessman called out from the comfort of his vehicle.

Abigael felt her stress levels rise as she wondered if she would be discovered and what she should do about it. Crawling back through the legs of the cattle with as much stealth as she could manage, she made it to the thorn tree bush and found a hiding place.

Bryan felt the fear of his wife being discovered. Chan, the businessman, did not know Abigael was on site or else he might have been looking for her too. But so far, his intelligence seemed to be based on old information. Chan's hit Bryan over the head with a rifle butt, and they were taken captive. Chan accused Thandi of selling out to the two white men. Looking him in the eye while trying to shake the blood away, Bryan said, "We are not here to get rich off the backs of the people. We have been hired to build a dam and supply water to the town."

"Ah, I see. You are a fool. A fool to think by giving these people water on tap, you will change their lives. Their lives are worthless. What benefit are they to the world? They live in the dark ages and do nothing with this valuable land. Animals roam where diamonds lie hidden under the soil. The crystal outcrop shows a greater wealth, only someone with money and power can access. And someone is going to be me when I get the signature from your friend, Thandi. And perhaps a photograph of us shaking hands over the deal. We would not want bleeding hearts around the world challenging my right to mine." Chan smirked at Bryan and shoved him to the ground.

Thandi leaned closer and spoke. "We must trust in my people to save us. Conserve your strength, my friend. It does no good to argue with a man with an eye set on a prize he shall never get."

Leaning down to sneer into Thandi's face, Chan said, "No one cares about this corner of Africa. No one will come and save you. The only reason you killed two of my men was because of the guns these men brought to the fight. What have you contributed? A few pop guns and knives? You are delusional, my lady, to think you can win."

And then, a feeling someone was watching them caused Bryan to look up and glimpse Abigael's face between the branches of the cattle pen. The sight of her made his heart sing and cry all at the same time. And she stayed. And stayed. As the sun rose in the sky, Bryan was sure Darren, the guard, would spot her, and she would become a pawn in the power game. As Chan instructed Darren and one of his other soldiers to release the cattle, he wondered how he could delay the inevitable. Perhaps allow Abigael to make her escape. Staggering to his feet, he said to Darren, "Can I have the cable ties removed from my wrists? And what about some water for my friend here? He is no good as a hostage if he is dead from thirst in this heat."

Darren looked at him for a moment and then nodded at Chi. "They will not escape with us all standing guard, so go on, give them some water and cut their ties."

Carl was way past the stage of caring and it was Thandi who leaned over him and dribbled some water over his lips. Bryan surreptitiously checked to see if he could see Abigael, but she was gone. The cattle bellowed and cried to be let out and the noise must have covered the sound and movement of her as she escaped. This insignificant victory gave him hope. One step at a time was all he could manage.

The three men moved around the cattle pen to the far side, where there was a gate allowing access from the outside. Taking his time, Bryan untwisted the wire of the opening. Chi was ready to help him with the cumbersome contraption the tribe's erected to keep their cattle wealth safe from predators. As the cattle smelled freedom, they surged forward, and Bryan and Chi stepped back before they were trampled. Darren laughed at their antics and stayed well out of harm's way.

Bryan was used to spotting wildlife amongst the foliage of the African bushveld, so it was not surprising he noticed the signs of the tribe hidden amongst the trees and grasses. Darren and Chi were not so well versed in bush lore, the lifeblood of children in Africa and did not see a thing. Darren prodded Bryan in the back with his AK 47. "Job well done. Now back to the village. We don't want Chan getting anxious."

Chi saw something out of place and called out to Darren. "I see a footprint, Darren. Should I follow it?"

"Yeah, why not? It beats sitting around looking at our navels all day long. We must be out of here by sundown to catch the helicopter ride to the ship, but until then, it is hunting season. See if you can shoot down a few tribesmen." Darren laughed at the thought and Bryan's blood ran chill.

Pushing Bryan in front of him, he reported back to the boss and told him Chi was off looking for a bit of fun hunting the people who scattered into the bush.

Chan too did not look concerned. His men were well trained and equipped with the guns his prey did not have. What could go wrong?

He walked back to see how his prisoners were doing. "I hope you have been thinking of your options, Miss Khumalo. The choices are death to all whom you love or wealth untold and co-operation with the likes of me. If it is not me who comes to mine the land, it will be someone else. Trust me. It is inevitable and I am offering a fair and equitable price for something you do not value and do not use." Chan waited for a response, but Thandi did not bother to answer.

Bryan checked on his friend and did not like the look of him at all. He was sweating and groaning as before, but obviously getting weaker. The blood stopped oozing from his wound and Bryan was not sure if it was a good thing or not. Thandi joined him as he gently removed the make-shift bandage from the wound. The skin was already inflamed and red and as Bryan washed the worst of the blood away; he knew his friend did not have long to live if he didn't get help. They needed to make a move if they were to survive. But with Carl unable to run, it was hopeless. Thandi shook her head at Bryan as he gently replaced the cloth over the wound to keep the flies at bay.

Darren was back on his perch on the hood of the vehicle and seemed to doze under a large cowboy hat and sunglasses. But even with Darren not doing his job, there were still the other men watching them. Four men sitting in the shade opposite them playing a card game and two men, wounded in the gunfight, were inside a hut, another two were fast asleep under a tree. But things could change in an instant and time was running out. Chi did not return by lunchtime and Chan became concerned.

"Darren. Send out two men to find Chi. Maybe the idiot got lost and can't find his way back?" Chan strode around the village. "And you four worthless individuals, stop playing cards and check the huts. See if anyone is hiding and if there is anything of value. Move, move, move."

They jumped up with alacrity and peered in doors. One man went right inside the hut he was inspecting and vanished. Bryan thought he saw a shoe as the man was dragged into the darkness of the hut. Thandi leaned over and whispered. "The women have made a hole in the back of the hut and been waiting for the opportunity to strike. Good on them."

Two more men disappeared in the same way before Darren became suspicious and called them all back. They were now down to five soldiers and the boss and of those five, two were injured. Darren went to the hut sheltering his wounded men and peered inside. Nothing. No sign of the men and no clue where they vanished to. He stood there for a moment with a frown on his face. "Chan, we have a problem. These black baboons have been stealing our men."

Chan came storming from the back of the vehicle to confront Thandi. Standing with his hands on his hips and anger streaming from him in waves, he said. "Tell your people to bring them back, Thandi, or else I will shoot Mister Bond in the leg. Now."

"Oh, my people do not want your men, Mister Chan. I will be happy to return them to you. In time. How many of them with weapons on them? Perhaps it is the guns my people want?" She smiled sweetly at the angry man. "And if you shoot my friends again, I will return your men to you in bite-sized chunks. And then we will see how confident the remaining soldiers will feel about their success against these primitive tribesmen?"

Chan struggled to control his anger and shouted at his remaining soldiers. "No one moves from this village. Do you hear me? No one. We can't afford for them to steal our men and our guns."

Darren said, "What about the two men guarding the construction camp? Should I send them re-enforcements?"

"No. Get them on the radio and ask for an update. I said no one leaves and I mean it. No one." Chan became angrier by the second as his control of the situation weakened. "Damn woman, why can't you be sensible and treat this land like a business? Idiot." It was not clear if he was referring to Thandi as being the idiot or himself.

Darren tried contacting the men at the construction camp, but there was no answer and Bryan smiled in delight at Thandi. They now had the upper hand. They used surprise and the men's complacency to their advantage and now all they were left to do was wait for the right moment to strike.

As the afternoon wore on, Bryan could see the tribe gathering in the shadows. Two more of the Chinese soldiers went missing when they went to answer the call of nature behind a tree. And then there were three. Mister Chan, Darren and Xu, a young soldier. Darren raided the arsenal and was now adorned with various incendiary ordnances and hand grenades strung on belts across his body. Mister Chan wore a Kevlar vest and a bullet proof helmet.

Thandi and Bryan lifted their heads at the call of a bird with no business being on this part of the land. The Fish Eagle call was haunting and penetrated the air with its clear tones. Thandi and Bryan looked at each other and smiled. This was the sign they waited for. The tribe was ready to strike. Thandi took Carl by one arm and Bryan the other and slid him under the vehicle. He groaned slightly, but nothing alerted Darren to what they were doing. A single shot rang out and Xu dropped to the ground with a hole where his eye once was. Thandi and Bryan rolled under the vehicle and pulled Carl behind one of the massive wheels, where he would be safe from any stray bullets. Leopard crawling to the other side, they waited for a second until Darren was distracted by a hail of fire from the trees, and then made a dash for the perimeter.

They heard explosions as Darren lobbed grenades into where he imagined the major force was holed up. But he did not consider the youngsters and their ability to catch and re-deploy the grenades into safer areas. Darren fought bravely, but the numbers were against him, and he was hit in the back by a well-aimed bullet. He rolled off the hood of the truck and onto the dirt with barely a sound. The ululations of the tribal women could be heard as he convulsed once and lay still. Now it was only Mister Chan who remained. He peeped out of the rear of the vehicle to see why the noise stopped and was confronted by Thandi's sister, Noni. She held her pistol straight in front of him, using both hands. "You have a choice, Chan. Death or dishonor?"

Emerging from the trees, the tribe came forward silently to observe this conflict. Jafari stood next to his mother as she held the Chinese businessman to account. "Dishonor is not an option. But then, neither is death." Chan lost his arrogance but not his belief in his ability to negotiate a good deal. "I will leave with my men and promise never to return. My honor will remain intact as long as no one finds out what has happened here. And I can live with it. Do we have a deal?"

Thandi stepped forward next to her sister. "We need it in writing, Chan. With perhaps a photograph to prove, we parted on amicable terms. And before you leave, you will set up a monthly payment to recompense the families of the dead boy and the injured so they can receive ongoing treatment." She looked over at the grieving mother of the herder. "A thousand dollars a month should just about cover it."

"What? Ridiculous. A funeral for the young man will cost nothing and a few herbs and poultices will fix the wounded. It's exorbitant. Never." Chan blustered.

"Oh well, we will have to invite the media in to document the atrocities you have committed and ask them to send copies of their reports to China. Would it suit you better?"

Chan stood for a moment looking at the ground and then said, "Sure, why not. I can afford a thousand dollars a month as long as I can write it off as a charitable donation."

Thandi escorted him to the back of his truck, where they went online and set up the automatic bank transfers. "And Chan, if you ever renege on your promise, well, I am going to make sure my photos of this incident are kept in a safe place. And I will instruct my lawyer he is to release them on my unexpected death."

Bryan and a very dirty Abigael cared for Carl. Bryan set up a drip of saline solution into Carl's ankle. Abigael dripped a protein drink into Carl's mouth and watched as he guzzled. His eyes still shining from the fever and pain, but his survival was now a possibility. Bryan re-did the bandage on the leg and clipped the cloth from around the wound as he cleaned and clicked his tongue in disgust.

"Stop clicking your tongue at me, Bryan. It doesn't help and I am not in the mood for sympathy." Carl complained.

"Sympathy? I should be the one getting sympathy, old friend. If I didn't try to pull your sorry ass out of the gunfire, I would never have taken the rifle butt to my head. Do you know I could have been happily in bed with my new wife if you didn't take it into your head to act like a superhero?" Bryan smiled at his best friend. "The wound is as clean as I can, with what I have on hand. Now if you can refrain from dying on us, we will get you to the hospital and the doctors can put anti-biotics into you."

They asked Amahle if she would accompany them to the town, where they hoped Carl could get the treatment he needed for his wounds. Bryan took the keys to the land rover and was climbing into the driver's seat, when Abigael took them from him. "No Bryan. You have a head wound and need your rest. Let me be the one to care for you now."

The Chinese men were herded into the back of their troop truck, which doubled as Chan's refuge and Abigael laughed to see Jafari standing guard over them as they climbed aboard. Paris stood between her mother, aunt and grandmother and waved to Abigael as they drove away. Everything was under control and now it was time for Carl to receive the care he needed. Amahle wiped his head with a wet cloth and even got him to drink a little water as the vehicle bumped along the road towards civilisation. Bryan touched Abigael's leg. "Thank you for being brave. You give me hope. And I have been praying all day this will not scare you away. I promise you this is not our normal lifestyle in the bush. Usually, it is the most placid and quiet job in the world."

They arrived at the small country hospital as the sun set and Abigael rushed in, looking for help. The nurse in charge took one look at this disheveled, muddy and obviously crazy lady and pressed the buzzer for security to attend to her and perhaps escort Abigael off the premises. But then Bryan walked in, and their attitude changed when they recognised him. He often brought ill and injured volunteers into this facility and they were welcoming in the extreme. Carl came in on a trolley and a doctor took a quick look at Bryan before handing him to the nurse to clean the cut on his head. Amahle and Abigael sat huddled on a bench seat while the men were attended to, and Bryan joined them. His head now sported a row of butterfly plasters giving him a debonair look.

"The scar is going to make you so much more attractive to women, my sweet. I will have to fight them off with a stick." Abigael smiled as she inspected the repair.

The doctor came out at one stage in the night and told them Carl was out of danger and receiving blood transfusions to replace the blood he lost. "He wants to speak to you Bryan." Looking at the woman and the girl, he said,

"Sorry, we can't let you in. Only one visitor at a time in the emergency room. Maybe later?"

Abigael and Amahle leaned against each other and fell fast asleep. The day stretched from drama to trauma and back, and fraught with danger. One of them killed a man for the first time and the other helped to save the children. A good day's work in anyone's book.

But life goes on and the following morning they woke to find pillows and covers laid over them on the benches. Bryan snored softly in a chair and the nurses tiptoed around them all. Carl was in recovery and laughed at the sight of his friends. "Oh Abigael. If only there was a camera. I hardly recognised you."

There was a small bathroom attached to his room and Abigael rushed in to see what the fuss was about. "Yikes. Why did no-one tell me I was still covered in mud and have messy hair?"

The nurse chased them out of Carl's room after a few minutes and Bryan suggested they go to the shops and buy some clean clothes and get a decent shower and a rest before returning. Which is what they did. They found a bed-and-breakfast place with two rooms to rent and lay down on crisp, clean beds. Amahle was much more impressed than the adults and whispered, "This is my first time in a hotel."

It took a week before Carl was ready to be released. The infection in his wound was surgically cleaned and Bryan and Abigael decided they would leave him in the gentle hands of a beautiful nurse who flirted outrageously with him. Returning to collect him after a few days, Bryan suggested they stay at the Ghost Mountain inn and wait for the bus to arrive with the volunteer tourists instead of having to make the drive the following day. Nurse Suzette frowned at them. "Why are you forcing him to go back to work? Have a heart."

But after promising to bring him back each week for a check-up, Abigael and Bryan loaded their friend into the Land rover and discussed the tasks needing attention.

"Suzette was a pretty little thing but thank you for saving me. Those four white walls were so depressing. At least at the Ghost Mountain inn, I can drink a beer or two. Beer is not something on the menu at the hospital." Carl stated, looking almost back to his old perky self.

As they sat at dinner, a woman wandered in on the arm of a very much older man. Dressed in a gorgeous silk dress, the other diners stared at the impressive sight. It was only as she passed them, they all realised who it was.

"Rebecca."

She turned to see who was greeting her.

Rushing into Bryan's arms and leaving her date, staring after her with his mouth open, she said, "Oh, it is good to see you all. I have missed you so much."

The man ambled over. "Let me introduce myself. I am Sol Leibowitz and Rebecca, and I are engaged to be married."

Abigael hugged Rebecca and whispered in her ear, "You know he is Jewish, don't you?"

"Silly you. Of course, I know." she replied quietly. "But he has oodles of money. Much more than Bryan. Oodles and oodles more. And he loves me. It's a win, win situation."

Bryan invited them to join their table and the night was spent chatting about Africa and the work Sol was doing. "Diamond buying and selling, old man." Sol intoned as he turned the ring on Rebecca's finger around for them all to admire. "If you ever need a bigger rock on your finger, Abigael, don't hesitate to call me. A friend of Rebecca's is a friend of mine."

Abigael looked at her grandmother's engagement ring, gifted to her. She said, "No. This ring survived the holocaust in Poland and is a gift from my grandmother, who survived the pogroms."

"Ah yes, it is worth more than carats for the tears shed for our people. You are a wise young woman. But if you want something for show? A dress ring to impress, then I am your man." He agreed.

No one mentioned the project in Makatini until they were eating an apple strudel with cream, when suddenly Sol seemed to remember where he heard Bryan's name before. "Didn't I see you being interviewed on Late Night Live a year ago? You are the two young men digging wells for people with no water. You were in the States looking for sponsors." When Carl nodded his assent, Sol continued, "When you are digging your holes, do you ever find diamonds or gold or maybe even platinum? I would be interested if you did. I could make it worth your while."

Abigael, Bryan and Carl almost fell off their chairs laughing, much to the surprise of their dinner guests. Sol pointed his spoon at Abigael. "What is so funny?"

"Mister Chan had this exact conversation a short while ago with us and our employer. Sorry, we don't mean to be rude, but it is not something we are interested in." Abigael stopped laughing as she saw the serious look on Sol's face. "This Mister Chan was very pushy and demanding. Some might call him assertive in the extreme. So, no more business dealings at the moment. No offence."

"Oh no, no offence taken. If you have met our esteemed Chinese gentleman, Mister Chan, then you have met the worst of my kind. I am sorry he has soured you on any other offers." Sol took out his business card and handed it over. "I am nothing like Mister Chan, I promise you."

After their guests left, Abigael handed Sol's card over to Bryan. "You can decide what you want to do with his information. But personally, I doubt whether Thandi has any interest in Sol's money or offer. It will be another version of the Chinese invasion into her land."

Bryan and Carl nodded agreement and they all went off to their beds for the night. The next morning, the volunteers arrived. All bushy tailed and bright enthusiasm. After basic introductions, they made the last journey to the Makatini flats. The enthusiasm waned about an hour into the trip. The group was spread over two mini-buses and Bryan and Abigael each drove one. Abigael and the engineers. She struggled with a language barrier between English and Norwegian until they struck on a subject close to all their hearts, machinery. Then all language barriers fell away and with much sign language and giggles, they made headway.

Bryan and the anthropologists in his van who asked non-stop questions about the history of the land until finally he suggested they Google their queries. When they got to the jobsite, the volunteers were stunned at the isolation and slowly walked around looking at all on offer. Carl was still on crutches and happily hobbled to his room and left the introductions to the site in the capable hands of his business partners and friends. The girls squealed with delight at the sight of the hammocks but frowned when shown the bathing facilities. The Americans seemed the most upset at the lack of privacy and Candy and Phoebe were very verbal and demanded something better be erected at once. Abigael smiled sweetly and then led them over to Thandi's village, where she showed them the very primitive lifestyle their neighbors were enjoying. They quietened down considerably and by the time they returned to the construction camp, appreciated what was supplied for them. But, to appease their sensibilities, Abigael said they could construct a small swimming pool as their first project. There was nothing like a taste of luxury to quieten the angry soul.

Abigael made sure they were supplied with all the plastic they would need and before the sun set, the engineers knocked in poles to delineate the edges. It was Bryan's suggestion as they sat around the pool at the hotel the previous week. He winked at his wife as she showed them the plans she had drawn up.

He sat back on a deck chair and observed the endeavor, laughing at Abigael and the way she bossed the youngsters around. "Use the spirit level. No, Basil, have you ever used a theodolite before? Well, give it here and I will show you how to use it properly."

"Candy, hold the string and twist it around the peg. Phoebe, put your back into hammering a peg in. It's not a marshmallow, it's wood and needs to be whacked." Abigael winked at Bryan as he sat in the shade. Carl came out to see what all the fun was about and started yelling along with Abigael.

He turned to Bryan. "I like the idea of name tags. Was it Abigael's idea? Why haven't we thought of it before?"

"Lars, come here and help me. Peta, can you drive a digger?" The instructions flew thick and fast and then it was time for dinner around a roaring fire. Some volunteers were co-opted onto kitchen duty and there was an array of salads along with the venison steaks sizzling away. Abigael plonked herself down next to her husband and punched him on his arm lightly.

"You could have come and supported me. I felt like a tyrant telling them what to do. Is this how it always is?" Abigael asked.

"No, not always. Often there is swearing, too. The first few days are the toughest and then they get into the swing of things and work like a team. We always try to blend the groups in the first few days with a joint project. And I have been wanting to see you in your bikini again. It's been too long." Bryan admitted.

Abigael leaned over and kissed him on the cheek. "We don't need a swimming pool. I am happy to wear it for you whenever you desire."

The swimming pool was a great success with the children of the tribe and Abigael organised swimming classes set up with Candy and Phoebe as the instructors. The two Californian girls were thrilled their skills were being used. And many of the young men came to offer their support when their work was finished for the day. Carl suggested it wasn't for the lesson so much as it was more about the view. She saw Candy eyeing Carl and Abigael poked Bryan in the ribs to alert him to the emerging romance.

"Nope, never going to happen. Carl has a strict policy of not sleeping with the volunteers. Each year we have a few who think they can change his mind. And each year he finds some way to avoid them. You watch and see. It's a master class in side stepping which I truly admire." Bryan smiled. "I have suggested he advertise for his own mail-order bride, and he says he is much too young to settle down."

"Isn't he the same age as you, Bryan?"

"Yes, we were at school together. But mentally, I think he still feels like an eighteen-year-old sowing his wild oats. Give him a year or two and he might change his mind." He leaned over and kissed his wife deeply. "Wild oats are not delicious when you have filet steak to enjoy."

Candy wore more and more revealing outfits each day until all the male volunteers flocked around her like bees to the honey pot. Some of the other women took her aside a week after they arrived and gave her a talking to about how to snag a man. Candy came out of the women's sleeping place the next day dressed in a khaki shirt and shorts showing not an ounce of flesh. Around the campfire, and Thorvald sat next to Candy. On the second night, he came bearing flowers plucked from the veld and Carl decided it was time for a bit of fun.

Carl announced, "Tomorrow we will have a campfire dance. Abigael will be in charge of music and Thandi has agreed to put on a tribal show for our entertainment." Turning to look at Candy, he said, "Can I ask you to be in charge of rounding up some talent amongst the volunteers? Juggling? Dancing? Singing? Or perhaps baton throwing is all acceptable. The only thing we frown on is nudity." He looked at Thorvald and continued, "You are to be her assistant and do whatever is required to make her happy."

Thorvald blushed to the roots of his blond hair and nodded in wild agreement.

The following day, the troops came to Abigael and handed her music to play or asked where they might find a special prop for their performance. Bryan and Carl made themselves scarce and Abigael wondered what they were up to.

Amahla and Jafari dragged big stacks of dried wood into the camp and Noni and her group helped set up lighting and seating under Abigael's instructions. Paris shook her head at her mother told her she could only stay for an hour. "But Mama, I am big now. Please." she begged. Finally, Thandi agreed to another hour, as long as Paris stayed close to Abigael all night.

As the sun sank and fairy lights twinkled in the trees, Amahla and Jafari swept the makeshift stage free of rocks and debris. Abigael noticed Bryan creeping into their quarters, and he looked very secretive. But she was much too busy to worry about what he was planning.

The fire was lit, and a huge antelope set up on a spit over some hot coals. Candy and Thorvald handed out printed lists to the performers and then waited for the entertainment to start. Bryan and Carl sat on either side of Abigael, and it was Thandi who stood up to start proceedings.

"Sanibona, my dear friends. The Gods have been good to us. The sky above us is filled with starlight and the hearts of those in this circle are abounding in love." She was dressed in her tribal robes and taking a carved stick, she pointed it at the four corners of the land. "From East to west and North to South, our ancestors watch over us. Tonight, we will honour them with our talents. We give thanks for good friends and fine food, for music and laughter. First, our young men will do a war dance, followed by our lovely young girls of the tribe. And then the floor is yours, my dear people. I declare this party started."

The drumming started as if from far away and built-in volume and intensity as the boys stamped their feet and entered the stage. A call was given, and they kicked their fur covered legs up so high, when their feet returned to the ground, the earth reverberated. Wearing isinene and ibeshu to cover their nether regions, they danced waving beaded sticks and small cow hide shields. The foreign volunteers cheered and clapped, and many took videos to send home to their families.

The girls were next, and their hips swaddled in brightly coloured towels and beaded straps. They outdid the males with their prowess and gymnastics. Finally, it was Candy and Thorvald who took center stage. Calling up first a couple who performed a swing dance with plenty of acrobatics of their own. Then a Scottish sword dance with fever tree branches instead of swords. The audience whistled and clapped in appreciation. When everyone who wanted to took a turn, Carl and Bryan stood up and held out their hands for quiet.

"Thanks to you all. For each one of you, we have a small gift. Made by the young women of the tribe, with a hidden gift courtesy of Carl and myself. Oh, and Abigael of course."

Amahla came in carrying a large shopping bag and bowed in front of Bryan, offering him the items. "No, no, you are part of this. Stay here. Paris, come and help your cousin hand out these gifts." Bryan suggested.

Paris jumped up and ran to do his bidding. Putting her hand out, she accepted a small woven basket from Bryan and then opened the lid and peered inside. "Oh Bryan, how pretty." Dipping her hand inside, she pulled out a crystal and held it up. "Sparkling stones."

Amahla took a few baskets and led her cousin towards the volunteers. "Give them to our guests, Paris." She urged. Silence reigned supreme as each person marveled at the amazing gift they received.

Abigael clapped her hands. "Dinner is served. Come and get it."

Thandi took a tired and happy Paris back to their village and volunteers and tribes people danced the night through. Abigael and Bryan joined in the joy. Candy and Thorvald seemed very cozy and there were certainly a few new romances started under the influence of the African sky. Carl danced with Thandi and Noni a few times before taking off for his own quarters. As the sky lightened and the sun peeped over the horizon, Bryan whispered, "You did well. I think our team is now united and we can get down to some proper business."

Abigael murmured, "Mmm. Do I get one of those cute little baskets? I would love to send some of them to my family as Hanukkah gifts this year."

"Sure. We can choose some next week. And perhaps a trip to the crystal fields for a walk down memory lane might not go amiss?" He suggested as he squeezed her derriere.

Abigael organised a huge breakfast for them all. Orange juice, scrambled eggs and toast, bowls of fruit salads and cream. And even though she did not partake of it herself, bacon, by the tray load. Those still awake laid around and talked of the most amazing night ever in their lives. "This will be a moment in my life I will never forget." Candy proclaimed as she snuggled in closer to Thorvald.

The anthropologists spent their days off wandering around the countryside recording stories and traditions. So, it was with surprise, one night, Abigael heard them discussing the recent stories they learned about a butterfly stamping its foot and destroying a garden. She listened as Peta said, "What do you think it means? Is there some

historical fact mythologised with this story? Was it
a local disaster? Or a global one?"

Abigael rarely interfered with the
students' private pursuits, but this was different.
Peta could be made the laughingstock of her
university if she went back with this saga. Abigael
ordered another copy of the Rudyard Kipling
stories after the attack and kept it in her room in
case a child wanted to hear it read again. Bringing
the book to the fireside, she laid it on Peta's lap.
"I think you need to read this. It will explain a lot
about the story of the butterfly."

The entire group were entertained by the
stories and took turns reading them out aloud.
The following night Bryan told them about the
myths and legends of the Fever trees and within a
week Peta sent in her thesis for her doctorate,
typed up and sent off for appraisal. She was so
excited about the way her research progressed, she
splashed it all over social media. Bryan's email
account was flooded with requests for places on
his next volunteer project.

Coming into their room, he scowled at
Abigael. "It's all your fault. I have universities
wanting to fund research trips and businesses
asking to pay for many odd things. I just cannot
keep up. I need a secretary to make sense of it all."

Lying back on the bed, Abigael said,
"What about Rosita? Her job in Namibia is almost
over and she is looking for a new challenge."

Bryan scowled at the idea of all this extra work when Abigael said, "And I won't be able to work at this pace for very much longer."

She waited for the penny to drop as Bryan turned to her. "Is this too much for you, sweetheart? Too hot, too many volunteers to control? I thought you were enjoying the work?"

"Oh, I am Bryan. I love it. But my shorts are no longer fitting me, and I need bigger shirts." Abigael admitted.

"Too much food? We can always have more salads and cut back on the desserts if you like?" Bryan asked with a quizzical look on his face. "You look gorgeous to me. I don't know why you worry about your weight. A bit more on the hips is fine."

"Oh, for goodness' sake Bryan, I am pregnant." Abigael laughed as his jaw fell open and he shook his head in confusion.

"How did it happen?" He asked.

"Okay. Let's start at the beginning. There is a daddy sperm and a mama egg and when a daddy and a mama love each other ...." Abigael started and then saw the smile spread across Bryan's face and she knew the penny had well and truly dropped.

"Carl, Carl. We have news." Striding across their bedroom, he grabbed Abigael off the bed and into his arms. Burying his head in her shoulder, he started crying, "It's great news. The very best of the best."

Carl rushed in to see his friend with tears streaming down his face. "Someone die? Not Grandma Rabinowitz? Not Mama Mary? Tell me. I can't stand the suspense."

Abigael opened her arm and pulled him into their communal embrace. "No, silly. You are going to be a surrogate uncle. We are having a baby."

Thank you

If you enjoyed this book, we would really appreciate it if you would leave a review.

You can also sign up to my newsletter. I do a fascinating blog where you can get a glimpse of my quirky life.

https://reshwity.wixsite.com/patriciapike